Marinello jammed his Colt against Eritrea's skull

"Okay," the *capo* snarled, addressing the man in black. "What's it gonna be?"

"Your head," the big guy stated flatly.

There was a tremor in Marinello's voice when he spoke again. "Suppose I give you this scum and we call it even, huh?"

"No sale," the soldier growled.

Suddenly the hostage gasped, "It's Bolan!"

Marinello swallowed hard and nodded toward the stoolie. "Look, he's yours."

"I repeat, no sale."

The mafioso's face registered stunned disbelief. "You'll kill him, just like that?"

The warrior shook his head. "No, you'll kill him, then I'll kill you. Just like that."

MACK BOLAN

The Executioner

DON PENDLETON's EXECUTIONER

MACK BOLAN

Shock Waves

A GOLD EAGLE BOOK FROM

W★RLDWIDE

TORONTO · NEW YORK · LONDON · PARIS
AMSTERDAM · STOCKHOLM · HAMBURG
ATHENS · MILAN · TOKYO · SYDNEY

First edition September 1985

ISBN 0-373-61081-5

Special thanks and acknowledgment to
Mike Newton for his contributions to this work.

Printed in Canada

If you cannot get rid of the family skeleton,
you may as well make it dance.
— *George Bernard Shaw*

The Mafia's closet is filled with unquiet skeletons
these days. It's time they learned to dance again:
a dance of death.
— *Mack Bolan*

To Sergeant Dominic Sansone
and the seven unidentified MIAs
returned by Hanoi on July 17, 1984.
Your war is over.
Sleep well.

PROLOGUE

The tall man moved through darkness, wrapping shadows about him like a cloak. Dark trees surrounded him and screened him from the traffic flowing even at this late hour on Fifth Avenue. A dozen strides from the curb, and he found himself in a different world.

It was a world habitually shunned by law-abiding locals once the sun set, a realm where predators held sway between dusk and dawn, but that did not intimidate the hunter. He was used to jungles, darker and more dangerous than this one in the heart of New York.

The Executioner had come to Central Park to keep a rendezvous, and he was early, taking his time along the footpath, making sure he had not been followed when he left the cab. He dawdled past the zoo, closed now, the night sounds of the animals inside completing the jungle atmosphere.

The predators in there, he knew, were under lock and key, secure. It was the human animal, outside the bars, who had transformed the once-majestic park into a place of dread, its name synonymous with mugging, rape and murder after nightfall.

He almost wished that one of them would find him, try lining up *this* mark—but he was on a different mission, and there was no time to spare. His contact, unaccountably, had picked the Chess and Checker House to be their meeting place. It was some fifty yards in front of him now, just visible between the trees.

At thirty yards, Mack Bolan spotted the waiting figure in the shadows, standing against the south wall, dragging at a cigarette held within his cupped palm. The glowing ember flared, disappeared, and flared again as Bolan started circling, a gliding shadow in the velvet black, diminishing the gap between them.

And he made the recognition ten yards out, despite the shadows. There was no mistaking that profile, the large but well-formed nose, dark hair swept back from the face in a modish style.

The men had never met, but Bolan knew his contact well enough from photographs—including mug shots taken over several years by agents of the FBI and the Baltimore Police Department. And he could have picked Nino Tattaglia out of a crowd any day of the week.

His contact gave a little start when Bolan showed himself, emerging from the shadows with a magician's slick timing. Hesitant, unsure if he was being set up for a fall, Tattaglia took his time about approaching, taking a last drag from the butt and flicking it away.

When they were close enough to speak in whispers, Nino glanced around self-consciously and said, "I'm Sticker."

Bolan took the hand he offered, pumped it once and gave the countersign.

"How's everything in Wonderland?"

Tattaglia relaxed—but only just. His eyes were constantly in motion, searching every shadow for a sign that they were being observed by enemies who might have followed either of them.

"You clean?" he asked.

"For now. We haven't got a lot of time."

"You called that right. I was afraid it might come down before you got here."

"So I'm here."

"Yeah, right. Well, anyway, the meeting's on as planned. Minelli's looking for a confirmation, as you suspected."

"And what about the opposition?"

"They'll be here, but rumor has it that Minelli's got a big surprise planned. Something that'll take the wind out of their sails and leave him sitting on top of the heap. I take it he's planning on a coronation."

"That must be some surprise."

Tattaglia's smile was devoid of mirth.

"Remember Dave Eritrea?"

A little graveyard chill swept along the Executioner's spine, and he nodded in silent affirmation.

"Well, according to the scuttlebutt, Minelli's got 'im, and his wife, to boot. He's sitting on 'em, waiting for the meet, so he can serve 'em with cocktails and take a few bows."

"How solid is your rumble?"

"I'm confirmed. My man in Wonderland reports their safehouse empty, recently abandoned. In a hurry, if you get my drift."

The Executioner was drifting with Tattaglia, sure, and he was damned unhappy with their mutual direction.

"What went sour?"

"No one knows for sure. They had some minor problems with the paperwork to start, but nothing recently. Could be they need a plumber down there."

Bolan read an understandable concern beneath the other's tone.

"You keeping dry so far?"

Tattaglia shrugged.

"I guess. Who knows? You do the best you can, and then one day some bastard pulls the plug."

And he was worried, sure, this man who had staked out a life along the razor's edge. For if the Mob could find Eritrea, despite his cover...

"How much time?"

Tattaglia did not have to check his watch before he answered. "It should be done this time tomorrow."

Right.

And time, as always, was an adversary to be faced and conquered with the rest, made hostile by its own unshakable neutrality. The clock ran down for friend and foe alike, and there was no escape once it had chimed the Armageddon hour.

"Where's the package?"

Nino frowned.

"Long Island, last I heard." He rattled off an address. "That was five, six hours back."

A lifetime, sure.

"What kind of guard?"

Tattaglia spread his hands.

"That's all I have, except the rumble says Minelli's got it safed. *Real* safe."

"All right. Can you get clear?"

"I wish. Don Carlos picked me special for the delegation."

Bolan frowned. "Some reason?"

Nino thought about it, finally shook his head. "No sweat. He likes me."

Bolan hoped the guy was right, for everybody's sake.

"Okay," he said, "I've got to move. Whichever way it breaks, stay hard."

"Hard, hell. I'm petrified."

They shook hands again, and Bolan left him by the Chess and Checker House, and moved in the darkness toward another rendezvous.

And this time he was flying blind, on a collision course, perhaps, with fate. He knew, of course, precisely whom he should expect to see, but as for *what* might lay in store...

The Executioner discarded his uncertainty at once. He knew precisely what was waiting for him on Long Island. It would be hell on earth, the usual, and any minor variations added by his enemies would be confronted as they came.

He had been down that road before and knew exactly where it led.

The terminus was death, for some—or all—concerned, and once you bought your ticket there was no disembarking until the final destination.

As for Bolan, he had seen his ticket stamped and canceled long ago. And he was riding, as always, to the end of the line.

1

"Remember Dave Eritrea?"

The question haunted Bolan as he made his final preparations for the probe, double-checking gear and weapons that could save his life.

And he remembered, sure.

The name, the circumstances of their meeting in New York, were stamped indelibly on his memory.

Eritrea had been an up-and-comer in the Mafia, intent on seizing power in the wake of *capo* Augie Marinello's fall, when he had crossed the Bolan path and come to sudden grief. The Executioner's command strike on Manhattan had upset Eritrea's plan...and very nearly trashed the "Black Ace" network, which comprised the Mafia commission's own gestapo in the process.

Nearly, but not completely.

As the coup de grace Mack Bolan had arranged for Dave Eritrea to be exposed as a stoolie, a role he had never played...until his shaken fellow mafiosi made it necessary. Already doomed, Eritrea had little choice but to accept the offer of a new identity, another life inside the federal witness program, as a trade-off for his vast knowledge of the Mob. His turning had been counted as a major coup in Washington, and Hal Brognola, manning things at Justice, had received the lion's share of credit for the victory.

But Brognola had known of Bolan's part, oh yes, and quietly, behind the scenes, spread the word.

Eritrea's conversion marked a turning point in Bolan's private war. The Mafia was reeling even before the *capo* made his move; when it was later caught between the Bolan hammer and Brognola's anvil, it appeared to be the beginning of the end for the brotherhood of evil. Bolan felt secure enough to listen when Brognola broached the subject of a wider war against a larger enemy, and after one last mile against the old familiar foe, the Executioner moved on to other battlefields.

But he had watched carefully for any signs of a resurgence in the Mafia, damn right, and more than once he had diverted from pursuit of terrorists to swat the *capos* down. Lately released from all official ties and sanctions, he had spent more time investigating what appeared to be a rejuvenated syndicate.

In Florida, where mafiosi had joined with Cuban-exile terrorists and agents of Havana's DGI, Castro's secret police.

In Hollywood, where drugs, sex and blackmail simmered in a rancid stew of politics and crime.

And in Las Vegas, where the old-line mobsters waged a brutal shooting war against invaders from the Yakuza.

It made good sense, of course, that these and other tracks would lead him eastward toward New York, but he had not expected anything like the Tattaglia bombshell dropped in Central Park.

He trusted Nino, knew from past experience that his intelligence was solid—even if delivered, as it sometimes was, with obvious reluctance. Nino was Brognola's man inside the Mob now, replacing Leo Turrin. Nino had been pressed into service with an indictment hanging over him for double murder. The alternative was to serve life without a chance of parole. Since Nino had turned informer, there had been nothing in his behavior to suggest duplicity on Nino's part.

He was a top lieutenant in Don Carlos Narozine's family of Baltimore, linked to every outfit on the eastern seaboard. His contacts had alerted him to "something big" in store when mafiosi from around the country gathered for their largest conclave in a decade, but the "something big" had taken Nino off his guard. So far, two people in the world outside the Mafia had been informed of the Eritrea scheme.

Tattaglia's first call, naturally, had gone to Hal Brognola.

And his second, at the big Fed's urging, had been patched through blinds and cutouts to Mack Bolan, via brother Johnny and the San Diego Strongbase.

It was time to move, and Bolan finished checking out his mobile arsenal. The warrior was in blacksuit, hands and face obscured by Special Forces war paint. Underneath his arm, the sleek Beretta 93-R was secured in its harness, built to accommodate the special silencer it carried. The silver AutoMag, Big Thunder, rode his hip on military webbing, and the canvas pouches circling his waist held extra magazines for both weapons and a selection of grenades. The pockets of his nightsuit held stilettos, strangling gear...the grim accessories of death.

Though he was going in with thunder, he preferred a silent probe to a violent confrontation. A quiet in-and-out would suit him fine, providing the hostile guns cooperated, and providing he found what he was looking for.

The Mafia safehouse was a rambling split-level on Long Island Sound. Its wooded grounds provided solitude, but from the terrace, facing westward, the Bronx was visible, and the speckled darkness of Connecticut farther north. It was the kind of view some people mortgaged lifetimes to secure, but tonight no one in the house cared about it. The focus lay within.

A sentry was posted in the front, another in the rear, but neither seemed much concerned about the possibility of meeting an intruder. It was the kind of duty that consumed so much of any soldier's time with watching and waiting, usually in vain.

He approached the front man from behind, looping taut piano wire around his neck while the guard was gazing at the stars. Bolan followed up with a twist and drag to throw the guy off balance as the wire sliced through his larynx, blocking his intake of oxygen and slashing his jugular. Then the Executioner rode him down, maintaining pressure while the blood spewed and the tremors faded, finally passing away. He used the slim garotte to haul the straw man out of sight beneath a hedge, and moved toward his second target.

Standing on a narrow pier that thrust out twenty feet or so into the sound, the sentry was staring distractedly across the calm obsidian water toward the mainland, heedless of the gliding death approaching on his flank. The soldier could have advanced upon the pier itself and been within striking range, but it was too damned risky. One sound, one creaking board beneath his feet, and nothing in the world would stop his target from unlimbering the stubby scatter-gun tucked beneath his arm. Then, no matter if Bolan won or lost the draw, the sound would rouse his enemies in the house and blow away his slim advantage of surprise.

He slid the Beretta from leather, eased off the safety, braced it in both hands and sighted upon his target, who faced away from him at a distance of thirty yards. Bolan lightly stroked the trigger, riding out the recoil to assess his shot. The parabellum mangler drilled a tidy hole behind an ear and expanded into bone and brain, its force contained within the gunner's skull. It lifted him off his feet and threw him overboard, the splash muffled by the wind rising off the sound.

Bolan doubled back to the house. He crossed the patio, its windows obscured by the curtains drawn across French doors, and circled around to a darkened window standing open to the night. Whatever else they were, the occupants were sloppy when it came to defense, and he was counting on that edge to see him through the next few moments.

Bolan pushed back the curtains, letting his Beretta lead the way inside. With a single fluid motion he cleared the sill, discovering himself inside an unoccupied bedroom. He reached the door and eased it open minutely, gun in hand, studying the corridor beyond. The sound of talking reached him.

"She's too damned old for me," one guy was saying.

"Yeah? So what the hell do you know, Junior?"

"Young or old, it's all the same," a third voice said.

"My ass."

"Could be. I haven't tried it yet."

In the ensuing chorus of hoots and jeers, he eased the bedroom door a little farther open, risking one quick glance down the hall in each direction. To the right, the hallway ran some twenty feet and ended at another door, evidently opening upon another bedroom. To the left, in a brightly lighted sunken living room, several gunners were lounging, their jackets off, revealing holstered hardware.

"We'd better get her ready," one of them said; Bolan ducked back under cover as an armchair groaned beneath the soldier's shifting weight.

"She's ready now," a second gunner chortled.

Bolan wondered if the troops were using alcohol to pass the time. It would not hurt his chances any if reaction times were down, the combat reflex slowed by liquor. Any edge was a welcome one.

A burly gunner passed before him, visible in profile through the crack of the open door. He waited long enough to let the hardman reach his destination, heard him fumbling with keys and chanced another glance along the corridor.

The parlor troops seemed oblivious to everything, caught up in the retelling of a story everyone already seemed to know. A fifth of Johnnie Walker was visible behind a bouquet of artificial flowers on the low-slung coffee table, and the sight gave him the impetus he needed to complete his move.

He left the cover of the doorway and glided toward the far end of the corridor. The other door stood open now, and while the gunner was no longer visible, his voice was crystal clear from just beyond the threshold.

"Up an' at 'em, momma," he said. "Time to take a little ride."

Despite his proximity, Bolan heard no response, and did not have time to wait. The sleek Beretta filled his hand as he slipped inside and silently closed the door behind him.

For just an instant, neither tenant of the bedroom sensed his presence, and he had the chance to size them up. The gunner was familiar, but nothing had prepared him for the woman, bundled in a sheet and plainly naked, who sat huddled in the center of the bed.

The hardman had her clothes all wadded up beneath one arm, and he tossed them to her. They fell just short enough so she would have to drop the sheet and reach a little.

"Get those on," he said. "I ain't got all day."

"You called that right," said Mack Bolan.

The woman gave a little choking cry and dropped her sheet, despite herself, but Bolan's eyes did not shift from the gunner. He saw the enemy begin to reach for the nickeled Smith & Wesson in his shoulder rig, knowing that the guy could never make it, knowing that *he* knew.

The 93-R whispered once, dispatching silent death to answer all the gunner's unspoken questions, and a tidy keyhole opened up between those staring eyes. The key was turned, releasing all his secrets in a crimson halo, bits and pieces raining down upon the lady.

The Executioner was at her side before the hollow man touched down, one hand pressed tight across her mouth to bottle up the rising scream. The numbers were already counting down like thunder in his head, and Bolan played a hunch, aware that everything was riding on his first impression.

"He was right," the warrior told her, nodding toward the corpse. "We haven't got much time. I need to find your husband, and the three of us can leave."

Momentary shock was replaced by understanding in her eyes, and he pulled his hand away to let her speak.

"He isn't here," she told him breathlessly. "They...took him away."

"How long?"

"Two hours, maybe more."

A hundred questions crowded Bolan's mind, but he was running in survival mode, and with Eritrea already gone, the number-one priority was crystal clear.

Get out of there and take the lady someplace where she would be safe until the storm blew over.

He retrieved her clothing, handed it across and nodded toward the open door of an adjacent bathroom.

"Get yourself together. We're on borrowed time already."

She was moving even as he spoke, sheet discarded on her short run to the bathroom. He pegged her as being in her late thirties, reflecting that she could pass for ten years younger in a pinch.

And Dave Eritrea was lucky.

The Executioner hoped that Eritrea's luck was holding, that it had not soured out completely. He hoped Eritrea was still alive.

Bolan meant to find him, but first things first.

And number one on Bolan's list was plain old everyday survival.

If they could make it safely past the outer guard, there would be time enough for planning further moves.

He double-checked the Beretta as he waited for the woman.

2

"Ready," Eritrea's wife remarked.

The clothes were rumpled, but they fit well, restoring a measure of the strength he had sensed behind her eyes. She had seemed vulnerable in bed, but now the look was resolute, determined. Still some fear there on the surface, naturally, but underneath there was tempered steel.

"They were about to take you somewhere," he said.

"Yes. I mean, you know as much as I do. No one's told me anything the past three days."

Wherever the gorillas had planned on taking her, Bolan did not mean to let them have the chance. The questioning would have to wait until they cleared the safehouse, and he doubted whether she knew enough to help him out.

Ideally, Bolan would have sought to bag a member of the hit team and question him at length, but the woman's presence made the idea tantamount to suicide. He had come here to rescue Dave Eritrea, and failing that, he would not risk Eritrea's wife on a misguided fishing expedition. Later, when she was free and clear, there would be time enough for gathering the hard intelligence he needed.

The windows were fitted with burglar bars, securely welded shut. Together with the locking door, they reinforced the prison atmosphere, confirming Bolan's first suspicion that the safehouse had been used for holding prisoners. They would need another means of exit. By the

time Eritrea's wife was dressed, Bolan had the mental
groundwork done.

The plan was simple: a little stroll along the corridor, de-
touring through the vacant bedroom, with an exit through
the window through which he had entered. No
sweat...except that they would have to make that stroll in
view of several hostile guns.

At least four gunners were left. While the Executioner had
bet his life on longer odds before, the variables were different now. He had the woman to consider, and even sloppy
marksmen pouring rapid fire along a narrow corridor had
decent chances of inflicting lethal damage.

The plan was risky, but sitting still was nothing short of
suicide. So that left no choice at all.

"We can't afford a sound," he told her, assured by her
nod of understanding. He was already moving toward the
door when it swung open in his face.

"Hey, Tommy, what the fu—"

The slender gunman never got it out. He was too busy
taking in the scene: his comrade, inert and bleeding on the
floor; the captive, dressed and ready to go; Grim Death,
decked out in black and swinging up an awesome piece of
hardware at his head.

Something in the gunner made him try, and Bolan had to
give him credit for the speed with which he ripped his
weapon from the armpit holster. Before it found a target,
however, Bolan's Beretta coughed, and 115 grains of death
penetrated the *pistolero*'s nose at fourteen hundred feet per
second. He collapsed immediately, his dying reflex trigger-
ing an aimless round that drilled the ceiling.

Startled voices called from the living room, demanding
explanations for the gunfire from comrades who were far
past answering.

"What's going on in there?"

When it seemed no answer was to be forthcoming, the
surviving gunners found cover and prepared for a siege.

The Executioner returned his sidearm to its rigging, drew the AutoMag and thumbed its safety off. The silent probe was over, and he needed thunder on his side if they had any chance of escape.

Another voice: "Goddammit, Tommy, Rico—answer up!"

He let Big Thunder answer for him, sighting on the sound and squeezing off, rewarded by a startled cry, a puff of tattered fabric from the sofa. Downrange, several weapons were unloading on him, angry hornets drilling through the bedroom door, releasing little showers of plaster from the walls.

A door sprang open on the corridor and unexpected company emerged into the line of fire. The guy had hoisted his shorts and drawn his gun before he left the bathroom, but drooping trousers slowed him. He glanced both ways along the corridor as if about to cross a busy street, then started to dash toward the living room.

Bolan helped him get there with 240 grains of screaming death between the shoulder blades. The impact threw him forward, spinning, and he picked up two more rounds from friendly guns before he sprawled facedown across the corridor. Infuriated, Bolan's opposition poured another concentrated fusillade into the bedroom, setting the door swinging on its hinges.

They would have to move without delay. A stationary duel was certain to result in death for Bolan and the female hostage while his enemies controlled the hallway. There was no way out but *through* the enemy, and Bolan knew that every moment wasted now was time which the hostile gunners would use to fortify their positions.

He ran one hand along his web belt, found a frag grenade by touch and hefted it, his eyes upon the no-man's-land beyond the door, calculating distances and timing. Satisfied, he pulled the pin, his grip securing the safety spoon, preventing premature ignition.

"Count to ten," Bolan told the woman, "then follow me. Go to the first doorway on your left, out through the window. Understand?"

Her frown bespoke concern.

"But you—"

"Forget me. I'll meet you outside. And if I can't...at least you'll have a running start."

She spent a moment mulling over Bolan's words and finally nodded grudging acquiescence. Bolan took the revolver from the dead thug lying beside the bed and passed it over to her.

"Anybody tries to stop you, think about your husband. Think about your life. Don't hesitate to use this thing."

She took the weapon and nodded. Bolan turned away from her, his mind already focused on the corridor: some thirty feet of carpeting, wide open, no obstruction except the body stretched across it.

No obstacles at all, unless you counted four guns, minimum, all trained down the narrow runway, aching for a target.

He braced himself, then pushed off, rushing through the open doorway, firing the AutoMag to keep the hostiles down and give him breathing room. He pitched the frag grenade and threw himself facedown upon the bloodied carpet, so he was half shielded by the body of the fallen gunman.

Peripherally, he saw the lethal egg land between the bullet-riddled sofa and an easy chair, then roll behind the couch. A bullet struck his human shield, then another and another. Counting down the seconds, Bolan prayed their aim would not improve. The thunderous blast rocked the parlor, shattering picture windows and bringing down a rain of plaster. Bolan hugged the floor as wicked razor fragments sliced over his head and dug into the walls. Then he was on his feet, already closing in before his enemies could pull themselves together.

One was stretched out near the sofa, fairly shredded, his shirt and trousers smouldering.

Another gunner, just barely alive, watched the Executioner's approach through his one remaining eye, the other having been messily removed by the razor shard that had also sliced open his profile from cheek to chin, exposing bone and teeth and sinew. He clutched an Army-issue .45 against his chest, as if mere contact with the weapon was some magic preventive against dying.

The *pistolero*'s single eye was fixed on Bolan now, and he was summoning his last reserves of strength to raise the .45. Bolan shot him from the hip at twenty feet and closed the cyclops's eye forever.

A movement on his flank alerted Bolan to the presence of the third and fourth contestants, and he hit a diving shoulder roll before their guns erupted. A pair of bullets flew over him, and then he was returning fire, Big Thunder challenging the other guns and drowning out their voices with its own.

His first round ripped the arm off the nearest gunner, spinning him around in an awkward pirouette. The second exploded in his face and picked the whirling dervish off his feet and propelled him against his comrade, both men sprawling to the floor.

Bolan's last round drilled the emptiness where the final gunner had been standing. The Magnum's slide locked open on an empty smoking chamber, and he jettisoned the useless magazine, already clawing at his belt for a replacement when the fourth man sighted down the vented barrel of a big Colt Python, straight into Bolan's eyes.

The Executioner saw his death in the cold steely eyes of his adversary, for at that instant he was no better than weaponless, the AutoMag's replacement not yet freed from its canvas pouch.

Suddenly the gunner stumbled, dropping to his knees. Someone had shot him.

Bolan and the wounded gunner swiveled to confront the unseen combatant, and both were startled at the sight of Mrs. Eritrea, revolver braced in both hands. She was aligning her second shot.

The gunner was fast, and would have been faster had there not been a bullet in his shoulder. His Python was almost on target when the lady hit him with a triple punch that kicked him backward, dead.

She held the firing stance until Bolan reached her and pried the .38 from her trembling hands. Then she turned away, no longer able to confront the dead.

"I owe you one," he told her softly.

"No. I couldn't let him...I..."

The tears were getting in her way, and Bolan left her to ascertain that their enemies no longer posed a threat. He was thankful she had disobeyed him. It was a twist of fate...and it had saved his life.

He fed the starving AutoMag another magazine, planning their exit. The hardmen had been preparing to evacuate when Bolan intervened, which raised two scenarios for his consideration.

If they had planned to take the woman out themselves, then the danger was over.

But if another crew had been dispatched to fetch the hostage, then there might be only seconds to spare.

"We're out of time," he told her. "Come with me."

"My husband—"

"I'll do everything I can, but first I need you safe and sound."

"Where can I go?"

"I've got a few ideas. We'll talk about it on the way."

He led her around the scattered straw men toward the entrance. She stared at his back as she followed, refusing to acknowledge the punctured corpses on either side. Outside, the night smelled clean, untainted by the acrid gun smoke and the smell of death. From behind them somewhere came the lapping sound of water beneath the private pier.

They had cleared the porch and were veering across the lawn when two pairs of high-beam headlights blazed to life directly before them, the glare pinning them at center stage. Bolan knew the transport team had arrived to collect their charge and carry her away.

The AutoMag cleared leather in a single fluid motion, rising toward the target as his finger tightened on the trigger. There was no time for speculation, no time for plotting strategy. He had to act instantly to preserve the slimmest chance of making good their escape.

He shoved the woman hard, propelling her beyond the circle of lights. Then the AutoMag roared in his fist.

Other weapons answered at point-blank range.

3

Ignoring the headlights, the Executioner squeezed off two rounds at the grill of the nearest Continental. Suddenly the hood was airborne, rising on a fiery mushroom, momentarily suspended, falling back across the splintered windshield.

It was no major fire—not yet, at any rate—but it was enough to distract the opposition, spoil their concentration. Bolan had moved on by the time a burst of wild, reflexive fire cut through the spotlit circle, searching for him.

The crew of the stricken Lincoln abandoned the vehicle, afraid that it would blow once the flames discovered fuel and traced it to the source. Secure in darkness, the Executioner was tracking the second tank, but it was rolling now, headlights extinguished, showing tail as the vehicle retreated down the driveway.

The Continental was still in range, but Bolan lowered his weapon and ran toward the trees and Mrs. Eritrea, waiting there in the shadows.

It occurred to Bolan that he did not know her name, that they might die together, any moment now, barely knowing each other. Yet they knew each other as only fellow warriors could. They had shed blood together, risked their lives in tandem...and it was not over yet.

He caught up with her, pulled her into the cover of the trees. At his back, the stranded crew was fanning out across the wide lawn, some twenty feet apart, weapons drawn and ready. They would approach cautiously, remembering the Lincoln and the roaring of the AutoMag...but slowly they would gather enough confidence and speed to overtake the runners.

Bolan knew that he would have to kill enough of them to make the rest turn back. He looked for the right spot, preferably as far as possible from his hidden rental car. The point he finally selected was a wooded rise beyond a narrow gully, where the high ground gave him an expanded field of fire.

If his pursuers were familiar with the grounds, they would slow down as they approached the gully, to prevent themselves from stumbling and plummeting headlong down the slope. If they were strangers there, then some of them might plunge ahead and lose their balance—or their weapons—in a downhill tumble.

Either way he would be waiting for them on the opposite side, commanding the high ground and looking down their throats.

He paused atop the rise, the woman pushing on for several yards before she realized that she was all alone and swiftly doubled back.

"What's wrong?"

"They're right behind us," Bolan said, exaggerating slightly for effect. "We haven't got a chance unless I stop them. Here."

She scanned the gully, seeming to grasp his intention.

"All right. What should I do?"

"Keep moving," he replied, ignoring the surprise and hurt in her face. He pointed through the trees. "Due south, straight line. Another hundred yards or so, you'll come to a wall. Wait there."

She swallowed hard.

"How long?"

He listened to the night...and to the sound of the voices calling back and forth to one another, drawing closer.

"Make it ten. If I'm not there by then, I won't be coming."

Bolan passed over the car keys, quickly told her where to find the car. It was a risk, of course, but he believed he could read the woman well enough to know she wasn't going anywhere without him...if she had the choice. If not...well, there was no damn point in stranding her along the highway with killers on the loose.

He shrugged, and as she departed he prepared to face the death squad approaching through the trees.

Bolan was a savvy jungle fighter, schooled in every aspect of guerrilla warfare—and he knew that it was practically impossible to enter any battle zone prepared. You could collect intelligence, run recons night and day, employ psychologists or psychics to predict your enemy's reaction in a given situation—and still you entered battle every time with doubt perched on your shoulder like a vulture.

Bolan found a vantage point, half sheltered by an elm, and eased the 93-R from its shoulder harness. Keeping his eyes on the gully and the trees beyond, he unfolded the foregrip and thumbed the selector switch to the three-round mode.

There were a dozen rounds remaining in the magazine, and more magazines where that came from. Plenty, right, to pin a fire team down and hold them in their place...or to annihilate them at the outset, if he played his cards correctly.

They were closing on him now, the pointman visible as a shadow among the trees directly opposite. He counted off another and another, shapes fanning out amid the undergrowth, advancing cautiously, as if they knew precisely where the gully was.

They were not strangers to this terrain after all. The darkness and the slim advantage of surprise would have to suffice. The gunners would expect him to be running instead of lingering to ambush them on the trail. Their caution now was due more to the topography, a need to keep their footing, than to a fear of meeting hostile guns.

He waited.

Bolan's one-time private armorer, the late Andrzej Konzaki, had equipped the 93-R with its folding foregrip, which allowed a two-hand firing stance, the left thumb hooked inside the oversized trigger guard to provide stability in automatic mode. Another extra was the combination of a sound suppressor with the specially machined internal springs, which effectively silenced the weapon. Throw in a cyclic rate of 110 rounds per minute in the automatic mode, and you were looking at one very lethal piece of hardware.

The pointman broke his cover, easing down the far slope, digging in his heels to keep his balance. On either side, the flankers were emerging now, secure in the assumption that their quarry would be running for his life, perhaps already gaining on the outer fence.

But they didn't know their quarry was Mack Bolan.

Planted atop the wooded rise, he watched gunners four and five appear a pace or two behind the rest. He sighted on each of them in turn, pivoting the gun from one to the next, then let it settle on the gunner on the far left, who was struggling to keep upright on the slope.

Split-second timing was the key, together with the kind of pinpoint accuracy that had been a Bolan trademark since the hellfire days in Southeast Asia. Left to right in one easy sweep: with a little luck he could take them all before they found his range and offered any serious resistance.

He framed the left-end flanker in his sights, squeezing off instinctively. The Beretta quivered in his hands as it dispatched its deadly messengers, and moved to the next target as the hardman stumbled and slithered to the gully's floor.

Alerted by a crashing in the undergrowth, the nearest gunner turned, a question on his lips, when Bolan's second burst ripped into his chin and answered all his questions for eternity. The guy fell, as if his legs had been jerked out from under him, and slowly toppled backward.

Number three, suddenly aware of something different, wrong somehow, was already jogging to his left and out of line when parabellum manglers took him in the side and shoulder, propelling him against an unyielding tree trunk. As he fell, the goon's scatter-gun discharged, alerting his remaining comrades on the firing line.

It was a race with time, and Bolan left the wounded gunner, tracking to the next target while he had the chance. The two remaining gunners were sprinting uphill, toward cover; Bolan chose the nearest of them as he emptied the Beretta. At thirty yards, the parabellums ripped across his target's pelvis, sending him sprawling, his legs suddenly paralyzed.

Number five was off and running as Bolan set the hot Beretta down and raised the AutoMag. Twenty yards was child's play for the silver cannon, even in the dark, and Bolan squeezed the trigger only once. The thunder rolled away from him and overtook his sprinting quarry in an instant, hurling him against a tree.

The Executioner scanned along his field of fire, examining the wounded and the dead. Of five, two gunners still showed signs of life, and Bolan spared the time for mercy rounds, the echo of his .44 reverberating from the darkened trees. When it was done, the soldier went in search of Dave Eritrea's wife.

And found her huddled near a hedge against the low retaining wall that partly enclosed the safehouse grounds. He startled her, but she recovered quickly, rising to greet him.

"Are they...I mean...?"

"We're clear for now."

He began walking and she followed. He helped her over the rough stone wall, and waited while she dropped down on the other side, then scrambled nimbly over. The rented car was parked near a stand of trees close by, and Bolan fired the engine, drove without headlights along a narrow access road toward the highway. As they reached the two-lane blacktop, he flicked the headlamps on...and knew at once that they were not alone.

The Lincoln that had earlier retreated was now approaching on a hard collision course, lights out, straddling the center stripe. The high beams flared, and the juggernaut began to gain momentum with a screech of smoking tires. Gun metal glinted in the interior as the tank accelerated toward them.

"Get down!"

She hesitated, freezing, and he shoved her beneath the dash, as safe as she would ever be in that situation. The AutoMag was in his hand, level with the dash. He floored the pedal, screeching toward a dead-end confrontation with the enemy.

He held the charger steady, mentally awaiting impact, knowing that a head-on at this speed would incinerate both cars, kill everyone. The smallest error on Bolan's part, the least miscalculation, and they both could kiss it all goodbye. And still, it was their only chance.

With twenty yards separating the vehicles, Bolan cranked the wheel hard left and veered across the narrow road, directly in the Lincoln's path. His tires were chewing up the shoulder, briefly losing traction, finally digging in, and they slid past with inches left to spare, the wheelman and his backup plainly visible, braced for the collision that appeared certain.

He had about a second to finish them off, and he opened fire with his AutoMag over the prostrate woman, her startled scream obliterated by its roar, all seven rounds unloading in the time it took to pass the Continental and skid to a stop along the shoulder.

He watched the tank roll on in his rearview mirror, saw the steering wheel lock beneath dead hands, saw the car swerve, go over in a barrel roll, spill its passengers, end belly-up across the highway. Then a glowing worm of fire traversed the undercarriage toward the fuel tank. When it blew, the Continental spun around and a lake of fire spread out across the wounded dinosaur, devouring its carcass and the writhing maggots sprawled around it on the pavement.

Bolan left them to their private hell, accelerating out of there before the woman could see. She had already seen enough, damn right, to last a dozen lifetimes, and he didn't feel she needed another lesson.

"That's three times now you've saved my life," she said as she regained her seat, "and I don't even know your name."

"LaMancha," Bolan told her, opting for the path of least resistance.

"I'm Sarah."

Bolan nodded.

She was safe for now. All the soldier had to do was drop her off, then go to find her husband. Find him and free him from whatever army had him under wraps.

Simple.

A piece of cake.

Like falling in a grave.

4

The telephone rang half a dozen times before a sleepy voice answered.

"Rafferty."

"I understand you're interested in Dave Eritrea."

The drowsy tone was instantly replaced by keen suspicion. "Could be, yeah. Who is this?"

Bolan smiled and said, "I'm a friend of the family."

"Oh, yeah? I don't suppose you could arrange an introduction?"

"Thought you'd never ask. I have the lady with me now."

"She looking for a place to stay?"

"Affirmative. You offering?"

Hesitation. Bolan could almost hear the mental wheels turning, scanners searching for signs of a trap.

"I'll have to make some calls. If you could meet me—"

"No good," Bolan interrupted. "She's bashful."

"Okay, I understand." A pause. "How did you get this number?"

Bolan played it cagey. "We've got some mutual friends in Washington."

"Uh-huh. Then I suppose you've got the address, too?"

"I'm looking at it."

"Yeah, well, give me a few minutes, willya?"

Bolan cradled the receiver, briskly retracing his steps to the rental and Sarah Eritrea.

"It's set," he told her.

"Are you sure?"

"I'm sure."

The Executioner had neither met Bill Rafferty nor spoken to him prior to this night's call, but he was sure. He knew the man by reputation, through Brognola's Justice contacts, and he liked what he had heard.

Bill Rafferty was currently a New York Police Department captain, placed in charge of the department's elite organized-crime unit. As a charter member of the city's tactical intelligence council, he owed his present post equally to sheer ability and some maneuvering by Hal behind the scenes. If any man had his finger on the Mafia pulse tonight, able to explain—and possibly predict—the furtive movements of the brotherhood, that man would be Bill Rafferty.

And he would be the only man who could provide a measure of security to Bolan's charge right now.

The captain lived in Queens, a modest home in Jackson Heights, not far from LaGuardia Airport. Bolan was a short drive away when he stopped to place his call. His knowledge of the man assured him Rafferty would listen and do his best to shelter Sarah Eritrea from the coming storm.

Whatever else he would or would not do depended on the man himself, and Bolan's method of approach. In this case, he decided that the only logical approach would be straightforward, open.

The soldier drove by Rafferty's home, seeing lights in the living-room windows, checking out the standard-issue unmarked police car outside and doubling back to park behind it in the driveway. He had taken time to change, to clean his face and hands of war paint, and the suit he wore above his hardware was expensive and stylish. Sarah Eritrea—still disheveled, but presentable—hung back a cautious pace as Bolan led her to the door and pressed the bell.

Bill Rafferty was dressed in shirt and slacks, complete with cross-draw holster on his hip, and he was in his stocking feet, his hair still rumpled from the pillow. Bolan thought he looked a boyish thirty rather than his actual forty years.

The Mafia expert scrutinized his callers briefly, Bolan first and then the woman, finally stepping back to let them pass.

"Come in."

He double-locked the door behind them, led them through a tiny vestibule that opened on the parlor, waving them to easy chairs and sofa. It would have been the family room in any other home, but Bolan's mental mug file told him Rafferty was widowed, childless.

"Coffee?"

"Thanks."

He disappeared, returning moments later with a tray laden with refreshments.

"Best I've got is instant."

"Fine."

The Executioner could feel the detective's sharp stare, knew that Rafferty had noted the Beretta in its armpit sling before he let them through the door.

The strike-force captain filled their cups and sank back on the couch to sip from his own.

"I had another call right after yours," he said, appearing nonchalant but watching Bolan for the trace of a reaction. "Seems they had a little trouble on Long Island. Some of Don Minelli's people bit the big one. You know anything about that?"

"I might."

"Uh-huh, I thought so."

"They were holding me," the lady blurted out. "He saved my life, and they were shooting, and...I mean..."

"Forget about that now." The captain raised a hand. "I'll bet you wouldn't mind a shower and some time alone, hey?"

Sarah glanced at Bolan who nodded.

"Great. Down the hall, first room on your left. You feel like sacking out, I've got two bedrooms. The spare's made up. It's down to the far end, on your right."

She cast another glance at Bolan and left them, disappearing down the hall. A moment later they heard the distant sound of water running in the shower.

"So, my friend, exactly what the hell is going on?"

Bill Rafferty sat forward, his elbows on his knees, cool gray eyes boring into Bolan's own.

"I helped a lady in distress," the soldier told him. "And I knew you'd want to see her."

"You already said that. Who's our so-called mutual friend?"

"The name Brognola ring a bell?"

And it was sounding inner chimes, all right. Bill Rafferty sat back against the sofa cushions, seeming to relax, but there was still a razor's edge of steel in every glance.

"How is Hal, anyway?"

"Still going strong, the last I heard."

"You're out of touch?"

The Executioner was cautious. He might trust Bill Rafferty with Sarah's life and with his own, in coming here at all—but Hal's security was something else again.

"We had a parting of the ways."

"I see."

Bolan wondered if he did. There was a glimmer in the eyes, almost as if the cop was looking through him.

The moment passed.

"So, what's your interest in our missing pigeon?" Rafferty asked.

"Rumor has it he's the main course on the menu at Minelli's coronation supper."

"Well, sure, it plays. Why not? A coup like that would win Minelli a whole load of prestige," the captain said.

"Enough to put him on the throne?"

"I wouldn't be surprised."

"You know they've got a meeting scheduled, then."

"I've heard some rumbles, but nothing solid."

"Call it firm. The sit-down starts tomorrow."

"You got an inside line, or what?"

The soldier smiled. "Or what. Brognola will confirm."

"Okay. Let's suppose they're running down another Apalachin. What am I supposed to do? This scum has rights, you know? Thus sayest the courts."

"I wasn't thinking of arrests. How about an informational exchange?"

Rafferty hesitated before answering. "I'm listening."

"All right. I know about the meet, who's coming—all the generalities. Before I move, there may be some specifics that I need."

"It sounds like you're ahead of me already, guy. What kind of move are we talking about?"

"Let's say the kind I made tonight, assuming I can find your pigeon."

"Well..."

"Okay, forget it. Keep a close eye on the lady, will you?"

"Dammit, wait a second. What you're suggesting is...unorthodox. I go along with this, my ass is hanging out a mile."

"That's right."

Another thoughtful pause. "I'll have to think about it."

"Fine. And in the meantime..."

"She'll be safe." He read the question in Bolan's eyes and added, "Here."

"All right."

"I'm working on the theory of a leak, myself. I've got it narrowed down, but..."

"No point taking chances," Bolan finished for him.

"Right."

The soldier rose, and Rafferty followed him to the door.

"You know, there's something—aw, forget it. Never mind. You'll keep in touch?"

"Bet on it."

Bolan left the captain standing in the lighted doorway, heard the door click shut behind him as he reached the car.

And Rafferty would think about it, perhaps contact Hal to find out what the hell was going on there in his own backyard. Brognola in turn would tell him what he could—and leave the veteran cop to make his own decisions.

As for Bolan, his decision had been made before he ever reached New York. He would pursue the enemy as far as possible. With any luck at all, he would be able to recover Dave Eritrea and make some substitutions on the menu for the coronation dinner, damn right.

As Bolan started the car, he was pondering the proper menu for a wake.

5

"Goddamn it!" Bill Rafferty swore.

The NYPD captain put down the telephone receiver, staring at the instrument in silence. He would have to make the call, there was no doubt about it, yet...

An image from the past was nagging at him, reaching out with spectral fingers from a shadowy corner of his mind, demanding that he recognize what was about to happen underneath his very nose.

"Goddamn it!" he said again, with more feeling this time.

When Bill Rafferty came home from Vietnam, he had been full of dreams: a wife and family, a thriving law career, success and wealth. His stint with the NYPD was a means to reach those ends, a way that he could make ends meet and gather some experience firsthand while he was finishing his studies at Columbia.

Except that something—everything—had changed along the way.

Elaine had been a part of it, of course, her death a turning point for Rafferty. The young patrolman's wife of eighteen months had been abducted from a shopping mall by members of a street gang, raped, beaten and left for dead within a mile of where her husband studied law and justice. She had lingered in a coma for eleven days and died without regaining consciousness. The doctors whispered to him that it was a mercy in disguise.

Bill Rafferty had not returned to Columbia. He put the dream behind him. In time, he earned the reputation of a cop who went the limit on every case. He had eleven righteous shootings on his record when he walked into the middle of a major drug deal one Thanksgiving night and routed the participants; they shot him twice, but when the smoke cleared, Rafferty was all alone among the dead—including one of Augie Marinello's crack lieutenants in the local family.

The shoot-out earned Bill Rafferty his gold detective's shield, together with a prestigious assignment to the fledgling tactical-intelligence unit. It also earned him Augie Marinello's personal attention, in the form of a contract on his head. A bitter war spun out between the two antagonists, and Rafferty killed three hitmen and jailed half a dozen others who survived their injuries before he built a solid case against the *capo* mafioso for extortion on the waterfront. The boss of bosses had been fleeing an indictment when he ran into a different kind of justice, losing first his legs and then his life in Jersey.

The week Mack Bolan came to town that first time, digging in for war against all five of New York's Mafia families, Bill Rafferty was working uniformed patrol. He had seen the grim results, helped scrape a few of them off the sidewalks. He heard the talk among his fellow uniforms: that maybe Bolan should be helped instead of hindered by police; that he was doing everyone a service and would be more deserving of a goddamned medal than a bull's-eye painted on his back. Bill Rafferty had listened, considered it and kept his private thoughts to himself.

And there had been some changes by the time of Bolan's second hellfire visit to Manhattan, when the gutsy bastard dropped in on a meeting of the Mafia's *commissione*, putting death on the agenda. Bill Rafferty was working on the strike force then, celebrating Augie Marinello's recent departure.

On Bolan's third and last appearance in the city, Rafferty was heading up the organized-crime unit, making some impressive scores against the local brotherhood. The newest captain on the force, he made no bones about the fact that Bolan's intervention had done much to pave the way, creating strife between the families and generating chaos at the top.

Bill Rafferty was not averse to shooting in the line of duty; he had done enough of it in Nam, and later on the streets. And he had put his licks in on more than one occasion when subduing a belligerent assailant. But the Bolan war was something else again, beyond the limits of the law, a deviation from the game plan on a scale so massive it was difficult to comprehend. Bolan's methods were effective, but they were wrong. Still...

When Rafferty had caught the bulletin on Bolan's death on a rainy afternoon in Central Park, a part of Rafferty had grieved. Not only for the soldier but for everyone—himself included—who would have to carry on against the enemy without a champion to take their part. It was irrational, he knew, but Rafferty had felt a sense of loss when Bolan died.

And when the news came through just recently that maybe Bolan wasn't dead at all...

The nagging ghost reached out, the fingers grazing conscious thought this time before Rafferty drove it back into the shadows.

He reached for the telephone, and punched up the long-distance number from memory. For a moment the clicks and hums filled his skull, and then he heard a muffled trilling at the other end. After four rings, a groggy voice answered.

"'Lo?"

"Get up. You're late for work."

"Like hell. Who is this? Rafferty?"

"I'm flattered, Hal."

"You're crazy, calling me at—what time is it, anyway?"

"Don't ask." Rafferty let his voice go serious. "I've got a problem here."

"Insomnia?"

"Enough to go around, unless I'm way off base."

A moment's hesitation on the other end, with background noise that told him Hal was sitting up in bed now, shaking off the cobwebs.

"Okay, shoot."

"I've got a part of what you're missing here at my place," Rafferty informed him.

"Oh?" The big Fed's interest was immediate. "Which part?"

"The better half."

"I see. You wanna fill me in?"

"That's tricky. The delivery man left your name as a reference. I assumed he must be one of yours."

A cautious silence at Brognola's end, and when he spoke, the man from Justice sounded worried.

"I don't have anybody up your way right now," he said. "There must be some mistake."

"Okay. And maybe I've got Snow White sacked out in my guest room, huh?"

"I guess you'd better start at the beginning, Bill."

He sketched the evening's strange events, omitting nothing. Then he recapped their conversation, leaving out his promise to consider what had plainly been a offer of collaboration in guerrilla war against the Mob.

When he had finished, Hal was silent.

"I think you may have trouble, Bill," Brognola said at last.

The captain snorted. "Great. So tell me something new, why don't you?"

"Right. I think you're looking at a full-scale war."

Rafferty frowned. "The families have been quiet lately...anyway, until this Dave Eritrea thing came up. I don't—"

The big Fed interrupted him. "I didn't say a gang war, did I?"

"Listen, Hal, if I was interested in dial-a-riddle..."

And it struck him then precisely what Brognola must be driving at. Before he could respond, the man from Washington went on.

"Let's see...I'd guess your visitor stood a bit over six feet, weighed around two hundred pounds. Dark hair. The face—well, never mind—but you'll recall the eyes."

"Goddamn it, Hal..."

"Precisely."

"You're supposed to be on top of this. I mean, why here? Why now?"

"Could be Eritrea." He paused, then said wearily, "Bill, I'm not on top of anything right now."

"That leaves me in the middle, huh?"

"Unless you pick a side," Brognola stated flatly.

"You're serious."

And Rafferty could not suppress a tone of wonder as he realized exactly what Brognola meant.

"I won't presume to offer you advice," the Fed replied. "I know what you'd be risking, and I know exactly what your visitor can do. The choice is yours."

"Some choice. I get to help him tear the town apart or just sit back and watch him do it on his own."

"There is a third alternative."

Of course.

He could attempt to bring the soldier in, alive or otherwise, before he had a chance to light a fuse beneath the city.

"What went wrong?" he asked Brognola.

"Say again?"

"Our visitor. I saw the mess that day in Central Park, when he checked out. Supposedly checked out. So who screwed up? And where's he been? I mean—"

"I know exactly what you mean. Right now, the bottom line is that you've got him in New York. He's yours for the duration."

"What about Eritrea?"

"I'll take the lady off your hands, don't worry. If you get a line on hubby—"

"Sure, I know. Just pass him on and let the bureau take the bows."

There was a brief pause on the other end as Brognola ignored the gibe.

"All right. About our out-of-towner. Is there anything that you can do?"

"I doubt it, but I'll check it out," the captain said.

"Thanks, Bill."

"No sweat."

The line went dead, and Rafferty cradled the receiver. As he slumped back in the chair, the captain of detectives realized that neither one of them had dared to voice the name.

Mack Bolan.

It was almost as if the act of speaking it could make its bearer appear, and Rafferty restrained an urge to laugh out loud. The guy had been sitting in his house as big as life—or death—and it was too damned late to worry now.

The soldier had arrived, and he had brought his own war with him, ready-made.

Where *had* the soldier been between that rainy afternoon in Central Park and the resurgence of reports that he was back among the living? Where does a legend go to hide? And what, in heaven's name, would make him take the hellfire trail again if he had found himself an exit?

Rafferty could answer that one, of course. The answer was commitment, to an ideal—a cause—and there could be no turning back on this side of the grave. The warrior was a true believer, devoting every fiber of himself to the eradication of the savages.

He was a living martyr, good only for killing and, in time, for being killed.

It seemed a frigging shame.

And Rafferty still had a choice to make, no easier than when he had decided to disturb Brognola.

He could hand over the woman, then sit back and watch the fireworks, doing nothing until it was time to sweep the streets of Bolan's carnage.

Or he could help. And risk his job, his future, indeed his freedom, in the process.

Choices. So many damned choices.

And whichever way he went, Manhattan would be in for war. There was no way around it now, with Bolan on the prowl and blood already shed. No matter what, the storm was here, breaking right around his head.

6

Hal Brognola leaned back in the leather easy chair, drawing deeply on his first cigar of the morning. Around him, the darkened study was already blue with smoke, but the big Fed didn't seem to notice. His mind was miles away now.

In New York. With Bolan.

Hal had discussed the briefing in detail with Nino Tattaglia before they made contact, of course. He had known what the soldier's reaction would be. Hell, he was counting on it.

And still it bothered him, this turning Bolan loose upon an unsuspecting city like some kind of doomsday weapon, then sitting back to catch whatever pieces might be thrown clear by the blast. They had been down this road more than once before, in the bad old days before the Phoenix team was formed, but now—well, it was different, somehow.

Bolan had been pardoned "posthumously" when he signed on with the antiterrorism force, his "crimes" officially forgiven by the President himself. The pardon was a secret, naturally, along with Bolan's new identity, his operations base sequestered in the Blue Ridge Mountains of Virginia. Everything about the war on terror, in fact, was so damned secret that the public never knew of Bolan's role...or that his part in the heroic effort had been terminated, tragically, by traitors from within.

Brognola stubbed out the stogie and waved away the smoke, rising and moving toward the window, beyond which a rosy dawn was breaking. But the world wasn't so rosy to Brognola.

The sky looked all bloody, the fleecy clouds discolored, tinged, like cast-off bandages.

It was already happening in New York. The bodies were piling up, and he would have to share responsibility for what was coming. He had helped to light the fuses, and when the charges started blowing in Manhattan proper, he would have to share the blame for the mangled souls.

It was a different game these days, at least for Hal Brognola. Bolan had not changed—would never change—but for a fleeting moment he had been legitimized, pronounced official, and his swift reversion to his former outlaw state had stunned Brognola.

For just an instant he was back in the smoldering hell-ground of Stony Man Farm, the stench of death in his nostrils. He could feel the deep abiding rage, the heartsick grief as he stood over the inert body of April Rose.

And he could well imagine what it must have been like for Bolan to lose the woman he loved and know that sellouts in his own backyard had called the play. The score was even now—as even as a killing debt like that could be...but there had been a price. Mack Bolan was outside the law again. Some officers were still reluctant to accept the news, but they were learning—in Miami, Las Vegas, Hollywood, San Diego.

It was looking like the bad old days, but with a vicious twist. In Bolan's first crusade against the Mafia, Brognola had cooperated in the hope that he could turn the guy around and make him part of The System. It had almost worked, but now the wild-assed warrior was back out there, and Hal was left with difficult choices in his absence.

He could cautiously lend a helping hand, let Nino and assorted others be conduits of information to the soldier, feeding him a list of targets for extermination. If it blew up in his face, he could forget about the almost thirty years he had invested in career and family, forget about his life, and bite the bullet like a man.

Or he could do his best to bring the soldier down, as he had tried to do so long ago, during Bolan's early war against the Mafia, before he realized that underneath the war paint they were kindred souls.

Uh-uh. He had come too far with Bolan to desert him now. He would never take up arms against the hellfire warrior.

They were in this thing together, albeit now on different sides of an invisible line. But they had walked that line before, and nothing said he could not learn the skill again.

And he had a chance to practice now.

New York would be a problem, certainly. The families there had gathered strength, repaired some fences since the Executioner had visited them last. The meeting scheduled to begin today had the earmarks of a major sit-down, possibly the largest since Miami.

If Don Minelli planned to crown himself the boss of bosses, the *capo di tutti capi*, then Dave Eritrea's head would be the perfect symbol of his power. He would eclipse the other New York families in a single stroke, and let the others know that he was now *the* power to be dealt with on the eastern seaboard.

Brognola knew that Minelli could pull it off and make it stick—unless somebody found a way to ruin it before he got the final pieces into place.

Somebody like Mack Bolan.

Another problem would be Bill Rafferty, an honest cop as devoted to his job as the soldier was to his private war. If Rafferty decided to reject the Bolan truce, if duty ordered him to intervene between the lone crusader and his marks, there would be hell to pay. Brognola knew that Bolan would not drop the hammer on a cop, but he had been in towns— New York included—where the law had issued orders for the soldier to be shot on sight.

He had known all that, and yet he could not say as much to Rafferty when they were on the phone. Rafferty had lived through other Bolan wars, knew well enough his modus operandi, and he would avoid an escalation of the killing if he had a chance.

Another problem in New York was Flasher, Hal Brognola's second undercover agent on the scene: he had lied to Rafferty, of course, about not having anyone on the scene. If their positions were reversed, Rafferty would undoubtedly have done the same.

But Flasher was a wild card in the game—unknown to Bolan, unknown even to Tattaglia. The agent's presence was a variable that could distort the whole equation. A time bomb for both sides.

There had been no reason to alert Tattaglia, and no safe way to clue the hellfire warrior in on something that his contact did not know.

Tattaglia was a born survivor. Flasher was a battle-hardened pro. And Bolan was a combination of them both.

Whatever happened in New York, the Executioner would meet the threat head-on, as always, with explosive force. If undercover agents crossed his path, they would be on their own. Survival of the fittest, and in the meanest jungle of them all.

Knowing he could not return to sleep, Brognola finally gave up trying. There would be something he could do around the office, certainly, if only staring at the silent, mocking telephone. In time, there would be word from Rafferty, from Flasher, from Tattaglia—from *someone*.

Whichever way it went.

And any way it went, Manhattan would be bracing for a firestorm. With all of New York's families involved, and dons from half a dozen other states arriving for the sit-down, the explosion would dwarf the blasts produced by Bolan's prior visits, create shock waves felt from coast to coast.

Brognola knew exactly what was going on in New York, no matter what he said to Rafferty. He knew the who and what and why of it as well as he knew anything on earth. The only open question that remained to haunt him now pertained to names of the survivors. And there was no earthly way to answer that one, not before the guns went off.

He wished them all the best. Bill Rafferty. Tattaglia and Flasher. Holy warrior Bolan.

He wished their enemies a living hell on earth before oblivion eclipsed them all.

He could do nothing to change the odds, nothing to alter whatever might be preordained for Bolan in New York.

Or could he?

Hal Brognola ceased his pacing and pounced upon the telephone.

7

Don Ernesto Minelli's retreat was located on Staten Island, overlooking Great Kills Harbor. Mack Bolan found the name ironic, almost prophetic, as he stowed the rental car beneath a stand of trees and locked it, moving swiftly back to lift a long bundle from the trunk.

Great Kills.

All right.

The place might live up to its name before he finished with Minelli and the other New York families.

A thirty-second jog brought Bolan to a hilltop overlooking the Minelli hard site, with a sweeping view of house and grounds, part of the harbor and the private access road that ran through gently rolling, sparsely wooded hills to terminate on Don Minelli's doorstep. New arrivals would be forced to use that road, unless they came by sea or helicopter and landed on the estate grounds. In any case, the soldier had them covered from his vantage point.

And arrivals were expected, Bolan knew, at any moment. Tattaglia had briefed him on the ETAs of seven *capos* coming in from out of state, and all would be arriving through the morning, driving in or chauffeured from the airport by Minelli's fleet of limos. Add the ranking New York bosses, and you had an even dozen of the nation's leading cannibals beneath one roof, a target Bolan could not resist.

But chief among the soldier's personal priorities was the rescue of Dave Eritrea.

He crouched in the shadow of an elm and peeled away the wrappings from his bundle. Nestled in the sackcloth was a Marlin Model .444 lever-action big-game rifle, fitted with a massive twenty-power telescopic sight. He raised the weapon to his shoulder, balancing the almost eight-pound weight of it in skillful hands, and leaned into the eyepiece of the scope.

Below, Minelli's house sprang into sharp relief, appearing almost life-size at a range of some three hundred yards. He scanned the grounds, picked out a hardman masquerading as a gardener out back, and knew there would be others in the house or among the trees, awaiting the arrival of their *capo*'s guests.

The rifle's magazine was already loaded to capacity with four of the big .444 magnum cartridges, each capable of delivering 675 foot-pounds of energy on target at the range he had in mind. Bolan worked the lever action now to chamber up a live one. Operating by touch, his eyes never leaving the compound below, he fed another round into the magazine, giving himself a five-shot capability.

And he would need it, oh yes, before the day got any older.

Two sleek Continental limos were approaching from the west along the private access road. If Tattaglia was correct, the first arrivals would be West Coast capo's Lester Cigliano and Jules Patriarcca, traveling together for convenience and as a symbol of their solidarity.

Based in Seattle, Patriarcca ruled an empire spanning the Pacific Northwest, with connections in Canada and along the Alaskan pipeline. Jules was considered *the* man in the West and Minelli would require his help—or, at the very least, Jules's tolerance—to stake out any Western claims.

As for "L.A. Lester" Cigliano, he was a newcomer, the surprised recipient of a battlefield promotion after his superiors turned up among the dead in Bolan's latest Hollywood campaign. Some said Lester was leaning heavily on guidance from the older, wiser Patriarcca and that Cigliano was a Patriarcca stooge, cooperating in the annexation of L.A.

Whatever else the two men had in common, they were vocal in their opposition to the East Coast hierarchy—and Minelli in particular—when it came down to sharing votes on *la commissione*. If Jules and Lester had their way, the rumors ran, there would be changes in the brotherhood from top to bottom to reflect the changing times, the westward shift in profit-turning rackets through the past ten years. Lately they had been gathering adherents in the families of the South and Midwest.

And so Minelli's sit-down could as easily become a showdown. Bolan would be counting on the everyday suspicions, doubts and paranoia that the average mafioso carried with him, and the Executioner planned to do everything within his power to heat things up inside the hostile camp.

Divide and conquer, sure.

It was a strategy as old as man, as old as war itself.

And Bolan knew it didn't really matter whether Nino had been accurate or not. He had a message for whoever was inside those closing limousines, one that would get to Don Minelli in a hurry.

He sighted through the scope, following the lead car as it cleared the trees and straightened into its approach toward the house. They would have passed through a checkpoint when they left the highway, and the private road was marked along the way by spotters on the grounds; they were running clear now, clocking close to sixty-five along the narrow track.

The marksman hurriedly worked out the trajectory and dropped as his finger found the trigger. At three hundred yards, his slug would be traveling just over eleven hundred feet per second—or some fifteen times the speed of his targets.

He took a deep breath, held it. Sighted. Squeezed. The Marlin bucked against his shoulder, and he rode the recoil, smoothly flexing the lever action, ejecting spent brass and chambering another round.

The bullet drilled through the lead car's forward fender into the engine block, which cracked like a slab of stone beneath a sculptor's chisel. Instantly the Lincoln's hood flew back, expelling smoke and steam, the driver blindly fighting with the wheel as the tank lost power, swerving, rumbling to a smoky halt some fifty yards along the track.

Behind it the second car was suddenly aware of danger, slowing slightly, then accelerating, swinging out to pass. It swung toward Bolan, providing a perfect target and the Marlin spoke again.

The tail car's left front tire exploded, collapsed into a wallowing rumble, the crew wagon slewing around in a half turn that ended when the engine flooded, stalling out.

The soldier marked a point dead center on the hood above the carburetor and fired another screamer, observing through the twenty-power as it found the hot spot. At once the crumpled hood was airborne, and flames were licking up from somewhere in the Lincoln's vitals as the doors sprang open, passengers scrambling for safety.

Bolan scanned the dozen frightened faces through his scope, recognizing Patriarcca and "L.A. Lester" Cigliano, who was beside Patriarcca, jabbering away. Their bodyguards fanned out, guns drawn, to form a tight defensive ring around the *capos*, searching for an enemy they could not see.

And Bolan froze, his twenty-power framing yet another face he recognized too well—Sally Palmer.

A former member of the singing, dancing Ranger Girls, she first had crossed the Bolan path in Vegas early in his war against the Mafia, and he had learned there was another side to the hottest lounge act in America. The girls were agents for Hal Brognola's Sensitive Operations Group, along with comic Tommy Anders and other unlikely players.

Bolan didn't know Sally's game, could not be sure if she had come with Cigliano or with Patriarcca, but it was enough for now to know that she was in the line of fire.

He scanned past Sally, past the shaken *capos*, settling the twenty-power on a hardman on the thin defensive line. There was no need to kill just yet. Perhaps an object lesson, just to put the wheels of thought in motion, set the West Coast dons to wondering who might arrange a hell-fire greeting for their benefit.

He gauged the drop and squeezed off, riding out the kick and staying with the target, kissing close through the telescopic lens. He saw the puff of fabric, spray of blood as slug met yielding flesh and fragile bone. The gunner wobbled, sat down hard, one arm coming up to clutch the ruined shoulder where the other dangled.

One round remaining in the magazine, Bolan worked the lever action, tracking on to find another target as the line of gunners wavered, broke. One guy was out of there already, sprinting for the house two hundred yards away. Bolan let the twenty-power follow him, already leading, then dispatched a thunderclap that tore his knee apart and sent him sprawling on the grass.

He caught a glimpse of Sally and the *capos*, crouched behind the stricken lead car, as he rose and backed away from there. It would not take the gunners long to get a fix on his position once they found their nerve. But he would be long gone before a strike team reached his vantage point. And in his wake, he would be leaving some unanswered questions for Minelli and his brothers of the blood.

The West Coast bosses would have questions of their own, bet on it, and their reception almost on the doorstep of Don Minelli's manor house would not endear him to Patriarcca or Cigliano. Already suspicious, they would be verging on absolute paranoia by now, and it might not take much of a shove to propel them over the edge, into outright hostility.

For Minelli's part, he would be wondering who dared to take such liberties on his land with his guests. If he ran true to form, he would begin by suspecting everyone and go from there.

The riddle of the moment, though, was Sally Palmer, and as Bolan reached his rental, stowed the Marlin in the trunk and turned the engine over, he was concentrating on the presence of the lady Fed in such rough company. It was a role she had played before, of course, and with success, but Bolan wondered just what strings she must have pulled—or what she must have sacrificed—to get herself invited to a major sit-down.

Before he reached the blacktop, Bolan knew that he would have to discover what she was doing there, find out if her mission was at odds with his or was simply one more piece within the larger puzzle. And in order to accomplish that, he would be forced to infiltrate the dragon's lair and have a close-up look at what was going down.

It was a deviation from what had started out as Bolan's master plan. But plans were flexible enough to change at need, providing that a soldier had the nerve and the imagination to effect those changes.

Bolan had the nerve, all right, and the experience to pull it off, but he would need a great deal more to come out the other end alive.

The Executioner was not a superstitious or religious man, but he believed in fate, some universal guiding force behind the endless war games men played out with one another. And while he knew for certain that right could fail and evil triumph, he could not help feeling that something in the "rightness" of a cause emitted an energy, a strength, which sometimes, subtly, changed the odds.

The white hats didn't always win, for sure, and he had seen too much hate and inhumanity enthroned to make himself believe that right makes might...but, then again, being right couldn't hurt.

The Executioner was going in, with courage and with experience.

To find a lady Fed.

To find some answers, right.

To find, perhaps, his death.

8

Don Ernesto Minelli surveyed the smouldering ruin of his limousine, wrinkling his nose at the stench of burned oil and rubber. The damned thing was a write-off, and he couldn't say much better for the second Lincoln, either. More than sixty thousand freaking dollars up in smoke, and still he had no firm idea of what in hell was going on.

"That's some reception you arrange for guests, Ernesto."

Patriarcca's voice was angry, but beneath the rage, Minelli heard a tremor of the West Coast *capo*'s fear. Beside him, Lester Cigliano stood with both hands in his pockets, glaring at Minelli as he fought to keep himself from trembling visibly.

"Hey, Jules...I'm sick about this thing, believe me. Thank the Lord it was a couple of my buttons who got hit, instead of you or Lester."

"Dumb luck. If I'd've known that I was going to a turkey shoot, I would've brought a few more guns."

"Same here," said L.A. Lester.

"Could be I oughta make some calls an' have a troop fly out."

Minelli did not like the way this was going, and he moved to head it off before it got out of hand.

"Relax, all right, Jules? I've got people on this thing right now. They'll get some answers for you, an' whoever pulled this shit is gonna wish that he was born without a trigger finger."

Patriarcca's silent scowl was like a slap across the face, and it was plain he did not think he had to look much farther for the author of the fireworks. Suspicious at the best of times, the *capo* of Seattle and his toady from Los Angeles were clearly thinking that Minelli was himself responsible.

Right now, Minelli had to find out who was lunatic enough to come in here, on his land, and draw down on his guests. When he had answered that one, then they could see to business, with some good old-fashioned entertainment as a lead-in to the main event.

As if in answer to his thoughts, a burst of static issued from the walkie-talkie carried by the houseman at his elbow. Don Minelli turned, waiting as the message was received.

"We've got some cartridge casings here," the disembodied voice announced.

The houseman pointed toward a rise about three hundred yards away where tiny figures stood between two trees in stark relief against the sky.

"Go on."

"Some kinda big-bore hunting rifle. Sucker must've used a scope."

"What else?"

"That's it. Five shots, five shells."

"Damn, give me that."

Minelli snatched the walkie-talkie from his houseman, fumbled for a moment with the transmit button, finally got it right.

"There must be something else," he barked.

The searcher's voice came back at him audibly tinged with fear and respect.

"No, sir. Nothing. Too much grass up here to hold a footprint."

Minelli fought an urge to dash the radio against the fender of his burned-out limousine.

"All right. But keep on looking, anyway. The bastard didn't float in here, for cryin' out loud."

"Yessir. Out."

The walkie-talkie hissed at him, went dead, and Minelli passed it back to his houseman. He forced a reassuring smile and turned to meet the scowling faces of his guests.

"They'll work it out," he said. "Don't worry. Anybody tries this shit with me is crazy."

"Like a fox," said the *capo* from Los Angeles.

Minelli's smile went stony, frozen on his face.

"I guess I didn't get that, Lester."

"Oh? Well, maybe I can make it plain."

But Patriarcca raised a hand to silence his associate.

"No more. It's hot out here, an' frankly, I'd feel better if we went inside. Whatever anybody has to say can just as well be said when everybody's here."

A grudging nod from Cigliano, and Minelli's jaw relaxed.

"You're right. Let's go up to the house and get some drinks, whatever. All your rooms are ready, an' the others should be here before you know it."

"Hope you've got a lotta Continentals, Don Ernesto," Cigliano gibed.

Minelli pretended he hadn't heard or understood. Patriarcca and his crony had brought three men each, together with the woman who stood beside Jules, watching everything and saying nothing. Too damn many for a showdown on the lawn, but if the skinny L.A. *capo* kept on needling him...

And why, in heaven's name, did something like this have to happen now, when it was most important for him to present the image of a man in full control of his surroundings? As he walked back to the house, trying to make small talk with his shaken guests, Minelli's mind was working on the riddle, coming up with nothing that made sense.

It seemed improbable that anyone intent on killing either of his visitors would do it there, so far from home, when they could easily have sniped them on their own respective turfs. A sniper with the skill of this one could have taken Patriarcca or his upstart colleague any time, and that made Don Minelli's problem all the more perplexing.

Had the shooter known exactly who was riding in the limousines? Or was he firing blind, content to pick off anyone he found on Minelli property?

Why had he settled for destruction of the cars, wounding a couple of Minelli's buttons, when he could have had the bosses just as easily?

Had he been looking for someone else? Perhaps Minelli himself?

Don Ernesto picked up his pace, suddenly anxious to be inside the house and out of the glaring sunlight. He felt exposed, vulnerable, and he cursed his faceless adversary.

Someone was trying to upset his plans, to sabotage the meeting that had been long months in preparation.

Someone.

But who?

It might be Patriarcca, certainly. Or Cigliano, though his mind rebelled at the thought of L.A. Lester laying out a plan without someone to walk him through it. Either way, complicity by one or both of Don Minelli's guests would perfectly explain their lucky break in slipping through the sniper's sights. And then again...

Five more out-of-town guests and the four remaining *capos* from New York were arriving soon, and any of them might be seeking to profit by disrupting the conference. For any dozen men, there were a thousand different motives, and he could never hope to single out a culprit from the bunch unless the enemy got overconfident and tipped his hand.

He glanced back, making sure everyone was keeping up, and saw the woman watching him through big designer shades. She smiled, and he returned it briefly, breaking off the contact as he concentrated on the house and sanctuary, closer now.

Jules must be losing it, to bring a woman with him at a time like this. She was a looker, but Patriarcca should have had the sense to leave his squeeze at home whlie he was talking business with the brotherhood. Minelli wondered if his guest was getting sentimental, even senile, with advancing age. It couldn't hurt if push came to shove, and certain action was required to cancel out his opposition vote.

Whatever, it was clear enough that he would have to keep an eye on his guests all weekend. None of them, including—or especially—those who had already pledged their fealty, could be above suspicion, now that violence had come out in the open.

He would know precisely who his friends and adversaries were before the meeting ended, and he would deal with both.

Minelli had a few surprises for his visitors, among them the disposal of a traitor who had done his best to blow the brotherhood apart. It should be entertaining for the troops, and it would win Minelli their respect.

But there was more in store for Don Minelli's guests. The ritual elimination of a rat would be the least of it, when he was finished.

Minelli frowned, decided he would have his men begin the excavation just as soon as it was dark. A grave or two, to keep their hands in, let them get in practice in case a greater number should be needed.

Better to be safe than sorry.

And if anyone was going to be sorry this weekend, it would not be Don Minelli.

THE GATEMAN WAS IN UNIFORM, but there were three more guns in street clothes, hanging back, leaning against the wall and scrutinizing Bolan coldly as his rental coasted to a halt and idled. The uniform approached him cautiously, and

Bolan noticed that the thumb-break strap securing his Colt revolver in its holster was unsnapped, ready for the draw.

"Yes, sir? Can I help you?"

Bolan shook his head disgustedly.

"Damn right. You can tell the three stooges to stand clear and let me pass. I'm late already."

The gateman looked confused.

"Uh...late for what, sir?"

Bolan let the shades slip down his nose an inch and stared across them, feigning shock.

"Late for what? Where the hell have you been, Clyde? The Arctic?"

"Sir—"

"You've got a frigging meeting going on in there, and I've got news for Don Ernesto. That's important news, you understand?"

The gatekeeper's face was reddening, but he controlled himself and played it by the book.

"I'm sorry, sir. There's been a little accident, and—"

"What?" Bolan stiffened, appearing to notice the distant pall of smoke for the first time. "Well, shit, it's started. Will you call your watchdogs off and let me in there?"

"I'm afraid I'll need to see some kind of ID, sir."

"Goddamn it!"

Bolan reached inside his jacket, noting as he did so that the nearest of the gunners in street clothes swung up a stubby 12-gauge, obliquely covering the new arrival from his place inside the gate. Mack Bolan passed a laminated card across, his eyes never leaving the shotgun.

"Tell Elmer Fudd I'm out of season, eh?"

The gateman stared at the ace of spades, then back at Bolan's stony countenance, and finally retraced his steps to huddle with the hardmen just inside. They looked at Bolan with a new respect now—and a new suspicion. The shotgunner lowered his weapon a fraction, and when the uniform came back, he had the leader of the team in tow.

This time the uniform stood back and let a flashy suit do all the talking.

"No one tipped us you were coming, Mr...uh..."

"Omega," Bolan told him. "Could be that you didn't need to know."

"Yes, sir. It's just that, well..."

"I understand." The soldier let his tone relax, however slightly. "Everybody's got a job to do. Right now, my job's inside there, and I'm late already."

"Yessir."

The suit passed his card back and stood clear, waving the other two gunners away from the gate.

"Go right ahead, sir."

Bolan powered out of there without a word of thanks, and he could feel their eyes upon him as he rolled along the drive. The passport of the Mafia's gestapo still had weight behind it, from appearances. At any rate, he was inside.

A group of businessmen were surveying the remains of the crew wagons, some of them turning to watch his approach, drifting instinctively into a kind of defensive perimeter, the cars at their backs. He braked to a halt and was out of the car almost before the engine died.

"How long ago did this happen?" he demanded of the nearest gunner.

"Five, ten minutes. Say—"

"All right, you'd better get this mess cleaned up. We don't want any other guests to get the wrong idea, now do we?"

The housemen were glancing back and forth at one another, clearly trying to take his measure, but only one could find the nerve to question his authority.

"I guess you're new around here, huh?"

"A lot of things are new around here, Slick. New faces, new ideas." He pointed toward the nearest burned-out Lincoln. "New problems."

"Uh, Mr. Minelli—"

"Has his own problems, right?" Bolan countered. "You want to disturb him with some simpleminded chicken shit like this?"

"I was jus' thinking—"

"Don't. I come up short on any thoughts, I'll let you know."

There was a snicker in the ranks, and the houseman flushed, glaring at one of his companions. But he was used to taking orders, deferring to strangers, and for the moment, at least, he was fresh out of questions.

"All right," he barked at the others, "let's get this cleared away."

Bolan returned to his car, fired the engine and maneuvered around the second Lincoln on his way toward the manor house. At fifty yards, he marked the gunners clustered on the wide veranda, and he slowed for the approach, following the drive around toward a parking area on the side. He wedged the rental between a Caddy and a bright red sportster, noting in his rearview mirror that one of the housemen had detached himself from the rest and was walking toward him.

He palmed the ace of spades and held it ready as the guy approached, suspicion written on his face, his jacket open to provide him ready access to the holstered hardware underneath. When Bolan flashed the death card, he was visibly surprised. It took an instant for him to collect his thoughts and give them voice.

"You must want Mr. Lazarus."

Bolan filed the name away and shook his head.

"Don't bother him. He's got enough things on his mind right now. I need to double-check security around your new arrivals."

"We've got everything in place," the houseman said, his tone defensive.

The Bolan sneer was withering.

"I just dropped by your outdoor body shop, all right? So cut the crap and show me where they're staying. Now."

The guy was clearly pondering an answer, but discretion got the better of his temper and he nodded, turning on his heel to lead the Black Ace around the great house to the rear.

Aside from Don Minelli's mansion, half a dozen bungalows were arranged around the grounds, connected by flagstone footpaths. Bolan had observed them through the sniperscope, but the buildings were larger than he had thought. And the would-be king of mob land could secure an army on his estate, damn right, if he was so inclined. Or hide a meeting of his fellow *capos* from the prying eyes of law enforcement, sure.

"The Cigliano party's here," the houseman told him, pointing out the nearest cottage on their left as they approached. "Don Patriarcca and his people are next door."

As he spoke, Sally Palmer suddenly emerged from Patriarcca's bungalow and set off toward the house with long, determined strides. Mack Bolan seized the time and brushed the houseman off with thanks, pursuing her along the flagstones, swiftly closing on her flank.

"One second, ma'am," he called to her.

The woman hesitated, turned, her face a study in curiosity and irritation.

"Yes?"

The soldier waited until he was close enough to speak without the houseman overhearing him.

"Long time no see," he said, flashing her a smile before his face went blank. "How's everything in Wonderland?"

9

The woman's first reaction was a puzzled frown, and then her eyes went wide behind the designer shades. She glanced around, marking the houseman as he retreated, watching for any other source of danger as she took a cautious step toward Bolan.

Sally Palmer had not seen the soldier since their last encounter in New York, before he shed his face and took another to resume the war on other fronts, but there was recognition in her eyes, damn right, and in her voice, as she addressed him in a whisper.

"My God, what are you doing here?" It clicked a heartbeat later, and her cheeks went red. "Goddamm it, that was you back there, with all the fireworks."

"Guilty."

"What's the big idea? I've been working Patriarcca for a year now, and you damn near gave him heart failure."

Bolan smiled.

"I'll bet his heart can stand a good deal more than that."

She hesitated, chewing her lower lip, the first hot rush of anger and confusion slowly cooling off.

"You're right, but dammit...I don't even know what to call you."

"Just as well. I haven't got the time for a reunion."

"Bastard."

"Definitely."

Sally's voice went soft, the cutting edge dissolved. "I...I've missed you."

"Goes both ways," he told her honestly.

"You owe me a briefing, soldier."

Bolan felt the smile growing and headed it off at the pass. The numbers were running, and he had pushed his luck already, just by being there.

"Another time," he answered.

"Sure."

"Jules must be getting soft in his old age."

"Don't you believe it. He just...likes me, that's all."

Bolan read the embarrassment in Sally's face, and in another place, another time, he might have reached for her and let her know he made no judgments on her way of waging war.

Sally was an undercover agent, using every tool at her disposal to complete her mission. If the skillful application of her sex, her charms, could get the job done, then she would have been a fool to let the opportunity slip by.

The lady was a pro, damn right. A good one. With her angel face, her dancer's body, she could infiltrate the hostile camp in ways the Executioner could never hope to emulate. And the intelligence she gathered, all the secret blows she struck against the enemy, were vital to the war at large.

He read a hint of the old self-contempt in her face, there and gone in an instant, and there was nothing he could do to ease her mind. It had to be enough that Sally knew he thought no less of her. That he respected—hell, admired—her for the war she waged against their common enemy.

"It's lucky that you're here. I may need someone on the inside," Bolan told her.

"Wait a second, guy. I'm strictly gathering intelligence, not playing smash and grab."

"There may not be a choice."

Her frown bespoke more curiosity than irritation. "You obviously know about the sit-down, right? So, what's the big emergency?"

He scanned the grounds, alert for any sign of hardmen drawing near, but saw none closer than the swimming pool, some forty yards distant. "It's more than a sit-down. Try coronation."

She nodded shortly. "Right. I've heard that. Jules and Cigliano aren't convinced Minelli has the makings. Some others are inclined to agree."

"How many of them do you think would change their minds if he gave them a sign?"

"That depends on the sign."

"Try Dave Eritrea."

The lady Fed went blank for just a heartbeat, but recovered swiftly, holding her poise. "Well, damn it!"

"Yeah."

"What happened?"

Bolan risked a casual shrug, his eyes still on the poolside loungers. "Something leaked. Who knows? The point is that Minelli has him now."

"That changes things."

He nodded. "Maybe you should take a leave of absence."

Sally bristled, her spine stiffening. "Forget it, Captain Chivalry. I'm in for the duration."

Bolan knew that he had touched a nerve. "Okay. But just don't sit too close to Jules, all right?"

"I'll make a note."

A couple of the gunners by the pool were watching with more than casual interest as the unfamiliar face made time with Patriarcca's girl. The Executioner was betting that Minelli's troops at large were not acquainted yet with members of the Patriarcca-Cigliano entourage.

"We've got an audience," he told her, raising one arm to point in the direction of the house. "I'm showing you the kitchen."

"And I'm showing you the gate," she said, giving him a dazzling smile before she turned away.

"Stay hard," he told the lady Fed's retreating back.

"You, too," she answered in a whisper, never turning.

Bolan backtracked toward his rental car, long strides devouring the flagstone path. When he was almost there, he saw the houseman who had spoken to him earlier walking toward him. The soldier did not try to outmaneuver him. Instead, he slowed his pace to let the other guy catch up.

"You can see Mr. Lazarus now," the houseman told him, drawing even.

"No time," Bolan countered gruffly. "I'm late as it is, and I've got two more stops before I meet the next crew at Kennedy."

"Well, say—"

The soldier turned on him, voice going stony in an instant. "Say *what*, guy?"

Instinct and training took over, forcing the gunner to pull back. "Uh, nothing, I guess."

"You guess right. I'll check in when I can."

He slid behind the wheel and turned the engine over, letting the houseman watch out for himself as he powered the rental out along the drive. The guy just stood there, dwindling in the rearview mirror, and Bolan knew instinctively that he had made the license plate.

So be it.

He had come this far, but the infiltration of Minelli's stronghold was a minor operation, carried out on the spur of the moment. The next penetration would require careful planning. He would need the cover of night, and man-made thunder on his side to clear the way.

The soldier wondered who he might have missed by not confronting Lazarus. It was an alias, of course, perhaps the handle of the highest-ranking Ace in residence. And if Minelli had one Black Ace in his camp there might be others.

It was an opening, but it could not be overused. As Omega, he had already stretched blind luck about as far as it would go before it reached the breaking point.

When Bolan passed this way again, it would be as himself, and heaven help whoever tried to block his way.

He reached the burned-out tanks and raised a parting hand to soldiers who were laboring to clear the drive. They were using a little tractor-mower to drag a blackened hulk across the grass, plowing furrows as they went. Bolan grinned, wishing he could hear Minelli when the capo saw their handiwork.

He reached the gate, but this time through, the gunners in street clothes scarcely glanced at him.

He let his breath escape between clenched teeth. So far, so good...but it was far from over yet.

He worried about the lady Fed inside Minelli's camp. She was a pro, but this time her job had brought her to ground zero on the Bolan firing range.

Bolan hoped that he could spare her when the showdown came.

It would be chancy, when all the delegates had crowded into Don Minelli's compound, beefing up the ranks of human targets. That much more difficult to spot the friendly face or two among the hostiles when the battle smoke was everywhere and there was time only to kill or die.

He would watch, also, for Tattaglia when it began. The soldier knew that failing health and trouble with the courts were keeping Carlos Narozine home in Baltimore, but he would still be represented by a team of crack lieutenants, Nino chief among them.

Yet another headache when it came down to marking targets in the midnight hour.

But he was mixing up priorities, and Bolan reined his thoughts in, focusing on first things first.

Like Dave Eritrea.

He still had no idea precisely where the former *capo* was sequestered, and he needed that much before he turned the thunder loose around New York. Eritrea was the key to everything, and if the Executioner fell short of that objective...

No.

He had already made Don Minelli and his West Coast guests suspicious of one another. In time, the same technique would bring him what he sought—or bring the house down trying.

Right.

In time.

The one commodity that he was shortest of.

And the soldier knew that there was none to spare as he accelerated in the direction of Manhattan and the predetermined target zone. If he could not find Dave Eritrea, he would turn the heat on where it mattered, rattle cages until something dropped out, right into his waiting hands.

The Executioner was blitzing on, and God help any savage in his path.

God help New York.

10

The rapping on his study door roused Don Minelli from his private reverie. He swiveled in the padded desk chair, scowling at the door.

"Come in."

Lazarus was muscular, six-foot-four, and handsome as a movie star. The face was understandable, of course, considering the fact that he had picked it out himself and had it customized to meet his needs.

It was a living, breathing mask, and sometimes Don Minelli felt that he could tap one cheek and watch the whole thing crumble like a shattered mirror, leaving Lazarus without a face to call his own.

The Black Ace found himself a chair and settled into it without waiting for an invitation, regarding Minelli across the broad expanse of desk.

"What is it?"

"We just had a visitor."

Minelli did not grasp the meaning of his words. "Explain yourself."

The mask-mouth curved into a patronizing smile.

"We've been invaded. Infiltrated. Compromised."

Minelli's stare was blank, and Lazarus continued.

"Some hero came right in through the front gate, past your guards. He showed an Ace and made them think he was one of mine. Dumb bastards."

"How are they supposed to know, the way you're in and out all hours?"

"Someone should have phoned the house."

Minelli had no good answer for that, and he sat silent, waiting for Lazarus to finish.

"A coupla soldiers spotted him out back, by the bungalows, talking to Don Patriarcca's lady friend."

Minelli raised an eyebrow.

"Maybe he was asking for directions."

"Maybe."

And the soldier's tone left no doubt to his skepticism.

"You think Jules brought muscle with him?"

"I wouldn't rule it out."

"Your own damn people?"

"Hey, you know the score. Since Pat and Mike, since Barney bought it, our communications haven't been for shit."

"That's reassuring." Don Minelli made no effort to conceal his sarcasm. "Would one of Patriarcca's people try to hit him here?"

Lazarus shrugged. "They didn't try too hard."

"What's that supposed to mean?"

"It means that no one on his payroll took a hit. You lost two cars, two men. I didn't see a scratch on Jules or Lester."

Minelli frowned, thinking it through, winding up where he started. "What's the point?"

"Could be anything. Disrupt the meet. Make you look bad. Give someone the excuse they need."

"Goddamn it."

Lazarus was staring at his steepled fingers, frowning. "Of course, there's another possibility."

"I'm listening."

"You've got more delegations coming in throughout the day. It could be any one of them. It might not be the Coast at all."

"So what about this phony Ace—assuming that he is a phony?"

Another shrug from the enforcer.

"Either way, he could be working for another family."

"You just said he was talking to the girl."

"Coincidence?"

Minelli snorted, rocked back in his swivel chair.

"We can't leave anything to chance. I want a hard eye on that bitch around the clock. She doesn't take a leak unless I know about it. Clear?"

The Black Ace nodded. "Done."

"I want a roving guard on the perimeter. No more surprises like this morning."

"I've got people on it now."

"As for this other thing, our uninvited visitor..."

Lazarus did not wait for him to finish.

"The gate's alerted now. He won't be coming in that way again. I've got my people on alert for any unfamiliar faces. And we got his number."

"What?"

"His license plate. One of our friends on the police department ran it through."

"So?"

"It's a rental."

"Shit."

The Black Ace raised a placating hand.

"I've got a man en route right now to check it out. He'll let us have a name within the hour."

Minelli shook his head.

"And what the hell will that prove, huh? You think the bastard left his name? You think he even still remembers what it is?"

"It's a start."

The *capo* glowered.

"What I want, goddamn it, is a finish. Everything wrapped up, no more loose ends."

"You'll have it," the Ace assured him. "It just takes time."

"We haven't got a lot to spare. And we can't afford any more fuck-ups like this morning." He swiveled toward the window, stared across the wide expanse of lawn. "If there's any more shooting around here, I want to do it myself."

He felt, rather than heard, the Black Ace rise from his chair. Lazarus was halfway to the door when he hesitated, turning back toward Minelli.

"There's nothing going on that I can't handle," he said.

Minelli did not turn to meet his eyes.

"I hope not," he replied. "For both our sakes."

Lazarus closed the door and the *capo* was left alone. He welcomed solitude, a chance to sort his thoughts and put the pieces of the puzzle in place. They were multiplying lately, getting out of hand, and it was a damned uncomfortable feeling, despite the soldier's best efforts to sound reassuring.

And Minelli wondered how long Lazarus would stay aboard the sinking ship if things went sour. Not much longer, he surmised, than it would take to pack a bag and throw it in the car.

Suspicion of the Aces was widespread within the brotherhood, despite their legendary faithfulness. They were a breed apart, conceived to serve *la commissione* directly, and as the syndicate's gestapo they had cherished secrets that made them more awesome, perhaps, than they actually were. Dispersed and badly shaken in the Bolan wars, they had regrouped, after a fashion, but the Aces were still not restored to their former station. More than soldiers, less than bosses, they existed in a sort of limbo, without official rank, and it was tempting to suspect that they might scheme together, plot to seize the ruling power for themselves.

It was a problem he would have to deal with, Don Minelli thought, when he was finally in charge. A weapon that could not be handled was a liability to its owner and should be destroyed for safety's sake. If he could not control the

Aces, bend them to his will....then they would have to go.
And permanently this time.

If Lazarus was right in his assessment, if communications were so bad that one hand never knew what the other was doing, then it should be a relatively easy task. If not...

The possibility that Lazarus was lying, for whatever reason, had not escaped Minelli. Anything was possible, and no one knew that any better than the *capo* for Manhattan.

He himself was living proof that miracles can happen. He had emerged from the ashes of destruction to conceive a dream of an empire, see it come within his grasp. And he could almost feel it now, could almost taste the fruits of victory. No man alive would stand between Minelli and his goal.

His time was coming, but he had not come this far by ignoring danger signs. If Lazarus could not pin down the latest threat, Minelli would be forced to do the job himself.

And there would be no shortage of suspects.

The Ace was right in pointing out that Jules and Cigliano could not be absolved without a second glance. The sniper's pinpoint accuracy, their amazing fortune, all demanded closer scrutiny before he wrote them off as the intended victims of a hit.

As for the others...

There were candidates right there, in Don Minelli's own backyard, among the other New York families. Frank Bonadonna. Tom Gregorio. Vito Aguirre. Giuseppe Reina. The first two were almost openly hostile toward Minelli's new expansion, and none of them, he knew, was above suspicion.

Bobby D'Antoni, the Jersey *capo*, was a friend. Or was he? He possessed the muscle to become a major problem if he underwent a change of heart.

Santos Bataglia, out of Boston, was at best a friendly neutral. That was fine with Minelli, as long as he remained that way. But might a better offer sway him, move him firmly into the opposition camp? It was something to think about.

Chicago's Paulie Viccarelli had some problems of his own, with the IRS, the federal strike force peering up his asshole with a spotlight. By rights, he should be too damned busy to initiate a war...but on the other hand, he might be feeling insecure enough to read a threat in Don Minelli's sudden growth. Another possible.

Vince Galante, the Cleveland *capo*, was a wild card, dabbling in business with the Jews and Cubans as if they were all his long-lost relatives or something. It was possible that he would move on their behalf or on behalf of other outside forces, to consolidate his strong narcotics base and open new supply routes to the south and east.

Jerry Lazia, boss of the Dixie Mafia with his base in New Orleans, was tight with Viccarelli and Galante in the smuggling of heroin, cocaine, you name it. He had as many Cubans and Colombians on the goddamn payroll as he did *amici*...and he was another wild card.

In sum, Minelli realized that none of the expected delegates was totally above suspicion. Any of them might harbor some hostility, turn thoughts to action, and if two or more were joining hands against him...

No matter.

The Manhattan *capo* dismissed it, secure in his belief that there was nothing they could do to stop him now.

He had Eritrea on ice to show them his connections were the very best. That he was able to succeed where each of them, in turn, had failed.

And if Eritrea was not enough, he had his clincher in reserve. The damn-sure winning card securely tucked inside his sleeve. When he had let them see the pigeon, when he had revealed himself for who he really was, they would not dare to stand against him, singly or en masse.

He ran his eyes along the line of trees, two hundred yards away across the lawn, and picked out tiny figures laboring with shovels there. Two graves...and it could be two dozen, for all he cared.

Minelli's hands were steady when he turned back from the window. No longer trembling inside, he knew that he was equal to the challenge he had set himself. It was his destiny to occupy the brotherhood's long-vacant throne as the boss of bosses.

It was his birthright.

And there would be last rites, yes, for anyone who stood in opposition now. The future was his. As for the rest, they were expendable.

Within the hour they would be arriving from the airport, from their homes around Manhattan and Long Island. Minelli would be there to greet them with open arms and welcome them into the fold. The wise and loyal among them would be going home when he was finished, after they had put their seal of approval on his coronation. The rest would stay to keep him company and beautify the grounds.

He smiled.

Tonight was his.

Tonight he would fulfill his destiny.

11

Bolan tested the fire escape, keeping his grip on the edge of the roof until satisfied that it would hold his weight. It was an eighty-foot drop to the alley below, with nothing but trash cans and overflowing dumpsters to break a fall. When he was confident the scaffolding would not collapse beneath him, Bolan released his handhold, started down.

The target was a South Bronx tenement, identical to countless others in the blighted neighborhood. Officially condemned, they were more or less abandoned, save for rats and roaches, homeless drifters, any one of half a hundred street gangs thriving in the squalid urban jungle. Others had been torched—by landlords, angry neighbors, someone— until the neighborhood resembled London in the blitz.

The tenement was owned by a Manhattan corporation that in turn was owned by Don Francesco Bonadonna. On its seventh floor, it housed a full-scale powder factory, devoted to the cutting and repackaging of heroin, cocaine and other drugs for retail distribution on the streets. The plant was one of half a dozen in the Bronx, and Bonadonna had at least as many in Manhattan, cranking out more poison by the kilo, day and night.

The target tenement was marginally protected by a local gang, the Mau Maus, who presided over three square blocks of wasteland like an occupying army. Bonadonna might have wiped them out as easily as stepping on a cockroach, but he chose instead to put them on his payroll and let them take the front-line risks and give his own *amici* breathing room.

Bolan reached the eighth-floor windows, crouching to peer through filthy glass, alert for any sign of sentries lurking there.

Nothing.

The soldier passed on, scrambling down the rusty steps, his Ingram MAC-10 ready to respond if he was challenged.

There would be no Mau Maus, Bolan knew, inside the cutting plant. They were too unpredictable to work around the lab, and any one of them might grab a fistful of the magic powder, try to force it up his nose before the gunners standing watch could turn him into dog food.

They would be the outer guard, and if they were around, they would respond to the sounds of warfare once his strike began. If they appeared, the Executioner would deal with them as ruthlessly and finally as he would any cannibal adult, and let them know, damn right, about the pain that went with playing in the major leagues.

He hesitated just above the narrow landing of the seventh floor, and he bent to check out the windows. Where all the rest were coated with grime, the panes of these few were painted on the inside, guaranteeing privacy. The soldier smiled, knowing he had found his mark.

He donned a surgical mask and double-checked the Ingram's safety, making sure there was a live one in the firing chamber and extra magazines were readily available. Unclipping an Army-issue M-12 frag grenade from his web belt, Bolan hefted the lethal egg, calculating range and angles. Then he jerked the pin and let it fall, maintaining his grip on the curved safety spoon as he leaned into the pitch.

The grenade shattered the blacked-out pane, long shards cascading down like broken stalactites. Bolan backtracked, scrambling up the stairs and hugging gritty bricks.

Three seconds later, a smoky thunderclap cleared out the other windows, raining glass and plaster on the alley below. A shudder gripped the fire escape, but Bolan was already moving, vaulting through the open window frame and dropping to a combat crouch inside, his Ingram tracking, seeking targets.

One of three long laboratory tables had been overturned by the blast, tossing to the floor beakers and retorts, a hissing burner, flame extinguished now, a snowy drift of heroin and coke. A drifting haze of smoke and magic powder hovered over all, reducing visibility to well below the danger point. You could OD in there just breathing, right, and Bolan homed in on the choking, gagging voices of his enemies as he moved out of the light.

A sudden movement on his left, and Bolan pivoted, the Ingram an extension of himself, already locking into target acquisition as a slender lab attendant lurched erect behind the upturned table. He was decked out in hospital white, his surgical mask dangling useless below his chin, the strap— and half an ear—clipped neatly by a piece of shrapnel from the frag grenade.

The Ingram stuttered, parabellum shockers opening the lab coat and the tender flesh beneath, before the impact punched his target out of sight behind the fallen table. For an instant, Bolan's muzzle blast had cleared a section of the fog bank, and he watched it close before his eyes like the evaporation of a dream.

Or nightmare.

A pair of gunners loomed before him, navigating by the sound of gunfire, probing with their handguns as blind men do with canes. They never saw Grim Death in front of them as Bolan hit them with a blazing figure eight and blew them both away.

A door banged open on his right, and Bolan swung in that direction, found himself confronted by a member of the Mau Maus. Long and lean, with scrawny arms and an outlandish Afro hairstyle, he resembled a B-movie alien.

But there was nothing otherworldly about the sawed-off shotgun in his hands, and Bolan took an instant to decide if he would live or die. The punk stepped in, and Bolan's Ingram zippered him from crotch to throat, slamming him back against the doorframe; he hung there for a moment, finally slumping into a death sprawl.

Panicking, a pair of lab attendants broke from cover, sprinting for the open doorway; Bolan chased them with a burst, saw one man stagger, clutching his side; then they vanished. Seconds later, barking pistols told him they had found the Mau Mau rear guard.

As Bolan left, he fed a new magazine into the Ingram. From his web belt, he withdrew incendiaries, dropping them along his track, among the bodies, scattered pills, the drifts of heroin and coke. He cleared the window and was halfway to the roof before the fuses sizzled to life and tongues of greasy flame licked out behind him, lapping at the masonry, devouring the lab.

The fire would not put Don Francesco Bonadonna out of business. But it would make him stop and think. Inevitably he would start to shop around for enemies, for anyone who might desire to do him harm.

And given time, the finger of suspicion would be aimed at Don Minelli.

THE TALL BLONDE SHRUGGED OFF HER BLOUSE, let it fall behind her. She wore nothing beneath it, and her breasts stood firm, the nipples aimed at Benny Spitteri's face.

"Tha's nice. Let's see the rest."

"My pleasure."

The pimp rocked back in his swivel chair, and wondered if there was another man in all Manhattan who got so much pleasure from his work. Forget about the numbers, running smack, the rest of it. For Benny's money, there was nothing that could match the ladies, and at one time or another he had worked the best.

He was the manager of New York's most exclusive whore-house, with a clientele composed of politicians, UN diplomats and businessmen who ranked among the top four hundred nationwide. A conscientious businessman, it was his duty to test each product before offering it for sale, to make sure that his customers were getting their money's worth. The rejects were passed to other houses or returned to the streets, and if it took him several trials to make his mind up, well, no one would ever say that Benny Spitteri had been less than thorough at his job.

Like now, for instance.

On the other side of Benny's desk, the blonde peeled out of tight designer jeans, then the panties, and stood before him, hands on hips. He shifted in his chair, attempting to accommodate the swelling in his loins, and beckoned to her.

"Over here."

She moved around behind the desk and did not protest as Benny made her kneel in front of him.

"So far, so good," he told her. "Let's get down to business."

"Mutual, I'm sure."

Actions spoke louder than words, and he could hear the tall blonde loud and clear.

"Hey, take it easy there. We got all day."

The first explosion rocked his office like a muffled sonic boom, the shock wave rippling beneath his feet. An abstract painting fell from the opposite wall, its glass frame shattering as it hit the floor.

Rising from his swivel chair, Benny shoved the blonde away. He found his zipper, tugged too hard, rewarded by the pain of pulled hair.

"Goddamn it!"

He reached the center desk drawer, pulled it open, and the damned thing kept on coming, spilling pens and paper clips and all that office shit around his feet. The little AMT .380

backup bounced once off his instep, disappearing underneath the desk.

"Goddamn it!"

Scuttling around on hands and knees, he angrily combed through the mess, finally found the little pistol and retrieved it. As he straightened up, his scalp made solid contact with the sharp edge of his desk.

"Well, Jesus H. Christ!"

Tears welled up in his eyes as he lurched erect, almost colliding with the naked blonde who was attempting to retrieve her clothes. He aimed a roundhouse at her head and missed by inches, cursing as she pulled back out of range. No time to settle with her now, as yet another blast ripped through the high rise, rattling the so-called soundproof walls.

The doorknob momentarily defied him, slipping through his sweaty fingers, but he got it on the second try and threw the door back on its hinges, banging it hard against the wall. For just a moment he was framed there in the doorway, glancing up and down the corridor.

Outside, the smell of smoke was powerful. An avid movie fan, the pimp immediately flashed on mental film clips from *The Towering Inferno*, and his blood ran cold.

He started for the stairwell with gun in hand, nothing on his mind now but survival. He was halfway there before he heard the third explosion, louder now, and closer. Benny Spitteri hesitated, racking his brain for an alternate exit, coming up empty.

And then, the gunfire.

Benny picked out .38s unloading in a panicked rapid fire, their rounds exhausted in an instant. Those would be his buttons, shooting windows out for ventilation, maybe blowing locks off fire doors to clear the way.

Spitteri was running when he reached the staircase, and he froze there as a cannon opened up beneath him, answering the smaller weapons with a voice of thunder. No shotgun, that. No weapon carried on the premises by any member of his staff. And that could only mean...

He started down, his legs leaden; he was very much aware the .38s were deathly silent now.

Benny never saw it coming. For an instant he was poised there, one leg raised to take another step, and then his kneecap suddenly disintegrated and his leg turned to useless rubber, and he fell forward on his face. He struck the banister, rebounded, and was airborne for a second prior to impact at the bottom of the stairs. The little AMT bounced free and disappeared.

The world was upside down, distorted through a looking glass of pain, and Benny heard the thunder now, reverberating all around him, telling him precisely what had happened. His lower body was on fire. When Benny tried to move, his muscles never got the message.

Swimming in and out of focus, Spitteri saw the giant coming for him, seemingly suspended from the ceiling. The specter was dressed in black, and he was looking down the barrel of the biggest goddamned silver handgun in the world, pointed directly into Benny's soul.

"I've got a message for your *capo*."

Benny tried to answer, finally discovered that his tongue was out of order, too.

The specter bent closer to him, making sure he could hear every word.

"Tell Don Aguirre he should watch his ass."

The looming shape retreated, leaving Benny Spitteri there to wrestle with his pain in solitude. He would convey the message, certainly, if he survived, and someone would be made to pay for what had happened there. His injuries. His buttons lost. The damage to Don Vito's pleasure palace.

When the message was delivered, there would be hell to pay, and someone would be picking up the tab. In spades. It would be entertaining to observe the *capo* as he collected on that debt, with interest due.

Before the pain and darkness took him, Benny Spitteri hoped he would live long enough to see the show.

THE HARLEM NUMBERS BANK WAS SET BEHIND a soul-food restaurant, accessible directly through the kitchen, past a guard, or through a private entrance from the rear alley. Bolan opted for the front, aware of sullen eyes that followed him across the room, the angry stares attracted to his whiteness like iron filings to a magnet.

He felt no prejudice within himself, except toward savages who made themselves his targets by their choice of lifestyle. If his tours of Vietnam, his campaigns in the urban hellgrounds, taught him nothing else, he knew that color—just like beauty—was only superficial. The good or evil in a person was what counted, and it ran soul deep.

There was a sentry posted at the door, outlandish in his purple velvet coat and wide-brimmed hat. The guard's eyelids were half shut, and he was attempting to look casual as he watched Bolan. When Bolan drew abreast of him, he moved to block the doorway, arms crossed, glowering.

"Say, man, what it is?"

"It's business, dude. Why don't you step aside?"

The Black Ace in his hand restrained the lookout from a hasty move.

"So, how I know tha's straight?"

"You wanna bet your life it isn't?"

Momentary hesitation, then the sentry shook his head.

"G'wan in, man."

He held the door and signaled to another sentry stationed on the other side. The Executioner brushed past them both and through a second set of soundproof doors that opened onto the bank itself.

Inside, the place was jumping. Betting slips were piled along a cafeteria-style table and were being sorted into smaller stacks by number, and at the far end, a couple of hard-eyed types were busily cramming bills into suitcases, scraping coins into deep burlap bags. Bolan moved toward the table, already spotting the banker, with his bodyguards in tow, closing on an interception course.

"Hey, what is this, some kinda open house?"

The soldier swiveled, pinned him with a stony eye. "Why aren't you ready?" he demanded.

"Ready? Hey, ready for what? Who the fuck—"

The Ace of Spades cut off his words as effectively as a garotte and left the banker sucking like a mackerel out of water.

"They'll be here insidea ten minutes," Bolan told him fiercely. "You're suppose'ta be finished."

"Ten minutes? Finished? What is this?"

"You mean you never got the word?"

The banker spread his hands. "I dunno what the hell you're saying, Mr...."

"Well, goddamn it. Someone was supposed to call." He made a show of glancing at his watch. "Forget that, now. We've still got time, if we get the lead out."

"Time for what?"

"You're being raided," Bolan told him flatly. "Feds. We have to get this bread out, like right now."

"A raid? You gotta be...they were supposed to let me know before they pulled this shit."

"Somebody blew it. Look, I don't have time to stand around and yap. You wanna bag this up, or would you rather tell the don to take it out of your allowance?"

The banker hesitated, finally nodded to the hardmen on the money detail. They packed up the Samsonites in record time and double-locked the bags, taking no chances. They were moving on to the coins when Bolan's voice stopped them short.

"Forget about the change," he growled. "Just pocket what you can and leave the rest. You've got...six minutes now."

"The bags—"

"They go with me," he told the banker, already hefting one, then the other, moving toward the alley exit.

The banker tailed him closely, red-faced, clearly worried now.

"Hey, I'm supposed to be in chargea that," he whined.

"So, whadda you want, a receipt?"

"Well, let's say somethin' happens..."

Bolan stopped ten feet short of the doorway and stood there, the heavy bags dragging at his arms.

"Okay. You take the full responsibility, I leave 'em here."

The banker thought it over briefly, finally shook his head, a nervous negative. "I guess I got enough to do."

"I guess that's right."

A cold-eyed gunner held the door for Bolan and he stepped through, glancing up and down the alley, veering left in the direction of his waiting rental car. He felt the banker watching him a moment, then the metal door clicked shut behind him and he was alone.

He almost chuckled, picturing the chaos back inside the bank as they prepared to face a team of nonexistent federal raiders sweeping down upon them any moment. It would take some time to realize they had been conned, and then the shit would really hit the fan.

But nothing compared to Don Gregorio's reaction when the news got home. It would be worth the ticket price to see the banker's face as he recounted his excuses for delivering a fortune to a total stranger off the street.

The Ace of Spades would raise some eyebrows, right, and set some wheels in motion where it counted. Tom Gregorio, like other ranking mafiosi, had survived through middle age by cultivating paranoia in his daily life, suspecting everyone and everything around him, always. He would be far beyond suspicion now, approaching apoplexy, and his rage would need a target, someone to absorb its grim, destructive force.

The banker would suffice for openers, but he was clearly not the brains behind an operation of this scope. The don would have to shop around among his many enemies to find a scapegoat, and with skill, a dash of luck, the Executioner might just be able to assist him in his search.

The game was getting dirty in New York, and there was worse to come.

Before the day was out, there would be dirt enough to cover all concerned.

And Bolan knew the only way to sponge the city clean, damn right, was through a bloodbath.

12

Bolan inserted the coins and punched a number from memory, keeping his eyes on the parking lot around him, the busy street beyond. A squad car drifted past, neither of its occupants giving him a second glance.

The phone rang half a dozen times before he finally got an answer.

"Yeah?"

The soldier recognized Tattaglia's voice at once.

"I'm calling for LaMancha," Bolan told him.

"Uh, he isn't here right now. You got a number there? I'll have him call you back."

He rattled off the pay phone's number, listened while Nino repeated it back to him. The connection was broken, and Bolan cradled the receiver, waiting.

It was a system of communication he had first worked out with Leo Turrin, when the little Fed was undercover in the brotherhood. So simple it was virtually foolproof, the technique let Bolan keep in touch with Hal Brognola's man inside, without attracting undue notice to the agent or himself. Within the next ten minutes, Nino would excuse himself and find a telephone he trusted, returning Bolan's call. If time ran out, it meant that he was unavailable for any one of half a hundred reasons, and the Executioner would try again later.

Eight minutes on the nose this time, and Bolan lifted the receiver on the first long ring.

"LaMancha."

"Right. It's lucky that you called. I've got a message for you from your uncle."

Bolan stiffened at the coded mention of Brognola. "So?"

"He had some kinda sudden business here in town. He'd like to see you, if you've got the time."

The warrior frowned. "It's tight. He have a place in mind?"

"The Cloisters. Said he'd be there till they close, in case you get hung up."

"I'll see what I can do. When are you going in?"

"About an hour. From what I hear, you're keeping busy."

"Trying all the time. You'll find some changes in the atmosphere around Minelli's."

"Yeah, I figured. There's a chill in the air around my place already."

"It should be heating up before too long."

"I'll dress accordingly. You do the same."

"Bet on it."

Nino broke the link and Bolan hung up, moving swiftly toward the rental car. His mind was racing, trying to extract the meaning of Brognola's presence in New York. He might be there to help, of course; it would not be unheard of. Or he might be there to warn the Executioner away, to head him off before his blitz proceeded any further.

Either way, Mack Bolan knew that he would have to meet with Hal and find out what was on his mind. He owed the guy that much, at least. But if the Fed was selling any more "portfolios," attempting to recruit him or, alternately, divert him from his course, the Executioner was going to walk away.

He never once considered that Brognola might have laid a trap for him at the Cloisters. Another cop, perhaps, but not Brognola. They had traveled down too many long and bloody roads together, butted heads on more than one occasion and remained the closest friends throughout it all. If there was any man alive who came as close to Bolan as his own surviving flesh and blood, that man was Hal Brognola. And there could be no thought of a betrayal by the man from Wonderland.

He followed Henry Hudson Parkway North, beside Fort Tryon Park, and took the single access road that carried him beneath a grassy overpass and north again, inside Central Park now, circling around the Cloisters.

Bolan found a parking place close by the entrance, dropped a dollar "voluntary" entrance fee in the collection box as he passed through the turnstile. The building was arranged around a square central tower, with most of the ground floor devoted to an open courtyard. On Bolan's left as he entered was the Treasury, with its priceless collection of art, the Glass Gallery, named for its roundels and stained-glass panels dating from the fifteenth century, and the small gothic chapel filled with effigies and slabs from ancient tombs. The main displays were all upstairs, and Bolan found Brognola in the Spanish Room.

"How's everything in Wonderland?"

"Ass backward. You know how it goes. So how's with you?"

"I'm keeping busy."

"So I hear. They're howling all the way to Albany."

"So soon?"

"Somebody's got a lot at stake on this one. They can't afford to see it fall apart."

"Minelli."

"At the very least. He's got a lot of friends."

"Some enemies, too, I'll bet."

"Safe money. You can't please all the people."

"Have you heard from Rafferty?"

"First thing. I want to thank you for the lady."

"Half a job. I'm working on the rest of it."

"Go easy, huh? We want him, but there's more at stake."

"Like Flasher?"

Brognola turned to face him squarely for the first time, lifting a quizzical eyebrow. "There anything you *don't* know?"

"Plenty. What's her job with Jules Patriarcca?"

"The usual. Preventive intelligence."

"Is he that big?"

"Could be. Seattle's done its share of growing since you busted Al Nyeburg's balloon."

"Might be worth looking into."

Hal frowned, a mixture of uneasiness and pure concern.

"Right now, Jules represents a major voice of opposition to Minelli. Throw him in with half a dozen others, and they've got the weight to block him, maybe tilt the axis westward."

It was Bolan's turn to frown. A realignment of the Mafia, a new and stronger coalition, was the last thing he had in mind.

"I don't think it will get that far," he said.

"You planning an appearance at the sit-down?"

"I need Eritrea first, if I can get him. After that..." He let the sentence trail away, unfinished, and Brognola didn't push.

"I hate this goddamned job," said Brognola.

"That's bull."

"You *think* so."

Bolan smiled.

"There any way of getting Flasher clear?"

"I don't see how."

"Forget it. She's all right."

A hollow feeling in the pit of Bolan's stomach mocked his words.

"You know," Brognola said, "this time next year, I'm looking at retirement."

Bolan smiled.

"What's funny?"

"You, retiring."

"Yeah, I know. But I've been thinking maybe I should go for it."

Bolan shook his head. "You're too damned good at what you do."

"Old Mr. Indispensable, that's me."

"So, give it time. You've got a year. Things may look different."

"They may look worse. It's never finished, guy. You know that much as well as I do."

"I gave up looking for the finish, Hal. It's strictly day to day."

"So tell me something, will you? How in holy hell do you keep going? I mean *how* can you keep pushing it?"

The soldier's smile was almost wistful as he answered. "No one ever said I had a choice."

"God*damn*, I hate this job."

"I'm late. I've got some other stops to make before the main festivities."

"Be careful, huh?"

The big Fed knew it sounded lame and shook his head disgustedly. "Hey, scratch that shit. You never learned what careful means."

"I'll see you."

"Yeah."

He left Brognola standing there, among the trappings of another age, and started back in the direction of his modern war. The enemy was waiting for him, out there on the streets, and there could be no cloistered hideaways for Bolan, not while one of them survived to prey upon the weak and innocent.

Who ever said I had a choice?

The war was in his blood, and it would be there, burning, driving him to action, every moment of his life until that blood was spilled out on the earth.

Brognola had been right about one thing.

The war was everlasting, stretching out beyond the barriers of time and space. It had been going on for countless centuries before Mack Bolan's birth, and it would certainly survive him.

But for now, this moment, one determined man could make a difference.

A man like Bolan.

All he had to do was try his damnedest, give his utmost to the cause, retaining nothing for himself.

And he would keep on trying, sure, until his time ran out.

If necessary, he would die trying.

13

Bobby D'Antoni drew deeply on the cigar, bringing it to life, and finally waved the houseman back. The sterling-silver lighter snapped shut close to his ear and then was gone.

"Awright, go on. So what's your point?"

The *consigliere*, Joe Marcellino, leaned across the table toward him, talking with his hands.

"I don't like all this shit that's going down next door, is all. I say it stinks, and this is no time for a sit-down, when they're in the middle of a war."

D'Antoni spread his hands and blew a cloud of smoke toward the penthouse-apartment ceiling.

"War? I don't know anything about no war." He glanced around the table at his *caporegime*. "You boys know anything about a war?"

They glanced at one another, shook their heads, gestures that rippled around the table, counterclockwise.

"People's gettin' killed," Marcellino told him, bending forward so far that his chin was almost scraping on the tabletop. "No matter what you call it, now, the shit is in the fan."

"So stand upwind." The *capo* waited until his under-bosses chuckled dutifully. "I don't see any blowin' our way yet."

"Why push it, eh? The meet's been waiting this long, it can wait another day or two."

D'Antoni bristled.

"Wait, nothing. Don Minelli's counting on me to be there. I give my word. I don't show up, somebody's gonna take it hard...and I don't want them bastards makin' any plans behind my back."

"Minelli, hmm..." The little *consigliere* made a sour face. "I never trust him. You're smart, you don't trust him, either."

"As far as I can see him, Joe. If he's got anything in mind for us, I wanna see it coming from a long way off."

One of the underbosses raised a hand.

"Yeah, Paulie."

"Hey, I think Joe's onta somethin' there, with this Minelli business. Nobody seems to know that much about the guy, you know? An' I been checkin' since this trouble started, too. Seems like his family is the only one not takin' any hits."

D'Antoni chewed that over for a moment, puffing rapidly on his cigar, his eyes screwed tight against the rising smoke.

"Okay. So, le's imagine that Minelli has a thing against his neighbors. Could be the best thing ever happened to us, if the five families start chasin' each other in circles. Could make for lots of opportunities across the river, there."

"Could make for lots of headaches, too," Marcellino grumbled.

"So, I keep my date with Don Minelli, listen close to what he says. I take along some extra muscle for security...nothin' threatening, just common sense. I don't like what I hear—"

The massive picture window on D'Antoni's left, overlooking downtown Newark, appeared to shiver momentarily, the center of it puckering as if an invisible finger was being poked through frozen cellophane. The illusion collapsed in the space of a heartbeat, along with the window, and everyone was scrambling for the far side of the room, all tangled up in chairs and table legs, recoiling from the shower of fractured glass.

Everyone, except Joe Marcellino.

D'Antoni saw his *consigliere* die, the gray hair lifting as a bullet took him from behind, the time-worn face exploding like a melon with a cherry bomb inside. His brains were on the table, glistening wet, and then D'Antoni felt the contents of his stomach coming up as he was diving toward the floor.

His houseman took a little two-step toward the shattered window, dropping the lighter, one hand inside his jacket as he fished for his side arm. He almost made it, had his hand around the weapon's grips when he was lifted off his feet and hurled against the wall ten feet away. He hung there for an instant, crucified, and when he slithered down, he left a crimson track behind him on the paneling.

D'Antoni heard the gunfire then, as distant as the street sounds coming up to him from twenty floors below. A big-game rifle, the bullets traveling ahead of sound; their work was completed long before the victim had a chance to realize he had been shot.

The *capo* wriggled on his belly through a littered mess of broken glass and blood. Overhead, the rounds were coming in with mechanical precision, smacking into walls, furniture and flesh with fine impartiality.

One of his underbosses broke from cover, stumbled, finally found his balance halfway to the door. He took two strides before a spectral fist struck him hard between the shoulders, driving him face-first into the floor. He crumpled there, his leaking body serving as a doorstop, keeping out the gunners who were hammering to gain admittance.

Almost as an afterthought, the sniper answered them with two rounds through the center of the door, big elephant loads blasting holes the size of baseballs and driving back the rescue squad outside. A voice was screaming in the anteroom, and Bob D'Antoni wished to hell someone would pull the plug on that one.

A ringing silence settled in above the battlefield, the stillness almost suffocating in the aftermath of violent death. It took a moment for the street sounds to return, and with them came the sounds of moaning, weeping, someone mumbling a childhood prayer.

D'Antoni used a high-backed chair to pull himself upright, keeping well clear of the window as he made it to his feet. He deliberately avoided looking at Marcellino, slumped across the table where he had been arguing effusively just moments earlier. The *consigliere*'s voice was still now, his throat spread out across the conference table, blood soaking through the carpeting.

Two others dead, one slightly wounded there, at least one other outside the door.

The sniper knew what he was doing and Bob D'Antoni had already missed his chance to bag him. He would be long gone by now.

But there was time to send the message back. Repay the debt with interest—if he only knew precisely who the sender was.

One way to find out would be to keep his date with Don Minelli. Show up at the sit-down right on schedule and pretend that nothing strange and lethal had gone on in his own damned home.

D'Antoni would be keeping his appointment, but he would travel with a full security detachment, and never mind appearances. If someone thought that he was being rude, displaying lack of trust, then they could take a look at Joe Marcellino, make up their minds for themselves.

And if it turned out that Minelli had a hand in this, if he was making moves across the river, to complement his earlier expansion in New York, then he was biting off a mouthful that would choke him.

The *capo* of New Jersey wasn't feeling generous this morning, and he wasn't giving anything away, not one thin dime or one square inch of territory to those hungry bastards in Manhattan.

They could have what they could take.

And anything they took from here on out would be across D'Antoni's dead body.

GIUSEPPE REINA WAS WORRIED. It did not show beneath his calm exterior, the sunlamp tan and cultivated smile, but on the inside, Reina felt like he was going to explode.

The town was going up in smoke around him, and no one he talked to seemed to have the first idea of what was going on. There had been hits already on Aguirre, Bonadonna, Gregorio...and the city was holding its breath, anxiously waiting to see who was next.

So far, at least a dozen lives had been snuffed out, and Reina drew no consolation from the fact that they were all low-ranking buttons so far.

Sooner or later, the hit team's aim was likely to improve, and he did not intend to be standing around like a human target when that happened.

Reina was expected at Minelli's for the sit-down...was already late, in fact...but caution was his trademark when it came to dangerous situations. Let the soldiers take the risks, as they were paid to do. The *capo*'s job, as an executive, was to protect himself at all times and keep the family running smoothly.

Minelli would be waiting for him.

So let him wait.

Survival was the top priority, and Joe Reina was a born survivor. He had come up from the streets, the hard way, having nothing handed to him like some other *capos* he could mention, who inherited their thrones and never knew what it was like to work for a living.

No matter what was coming down, he would be ready when the shit storm reached his doorstep.

Preparedness, he knew, was half the battle.

Downstairs, half a dozen of his soldiers would be finished bringing up the cars, securing the sidewalk for his speedy exit from the high rise. He would be exposed for only seconds, but he was not taking any chances. Four tall bodycocks would flank him, two of them with stout umbrellas raised...in case some smart-ass with a rifle might decide to bag himself a *capo* from the rooftops.

Once he reached the cars, it would be milk and honey all the way to Don Minelli's hideaway, and they would all be safer there.

Or would they?

A frown creased Reina's brow, his mind returning to the problem that had plagued him through the morning, as the battlefield reports came in from every corner of the city.

What was Don Minelli doing all this time, while his *amici* were taking it in the teeth? Presumably, he would be making ready for the sit-down, welcoming out-of-town guests at his home, but then again...

The Mafia mentality could not resist the obvious suspicion, putting two and two together in some new and unexpected ways. Was Don Minelli's meeting somehow linked to all the recent trouble?

And if not, then who?

There was a lengthy list of possibles, and Reina could be certain only of his personal innocence. It could be an aggressive move by troops from out of state or even by another of the New York *capos*.

Except that all of them had been hit so far.

Except Minelli. And Reina.

The process of elimination was a simple one. Reina knew that he was not involved; that left Minelli, or...

He gave it up. A lifetime in the brotherhood had taught him that there was no end to possibilities for treachery. It was a waiting game of watch and learn from here on in. Unfortunately, the price of knowledge was climbing all the time. In cash. In lives. In time away from paying business.

And it was time to go. The cars were ready, and Reina steeled himself for the short hike through open daylight, his moment in the sun. The tremor made him smile, and he chided himself silently, realizing that he was behaving as an old man might, afraid to walk downtown and cash his frigging welfare check because the little boys who hung around the corners might be waiting for him.

Bullshit.

Giuseppe Reina feared no man, no army. He had an army of his own, and they had proved themselves in battle more than once. If anyone should be afraid, it was the bastard who would dare to challenge Don Reina on his own home turf.

He rode the elevator down with gunners all around him taking up the space and forcing civilians on the other floors they passed to wait and catch a different car. No point in taking chances with the smiling girl-next-door type who might be carrying a pistol in her handbag or the faggy-looking character whose briefcase might contain explosives, a machine gun, anything.

If Reina recognized that he was paranoid, it did not bother him. His paranoia was no more than a survival tool, essential in the urban jungle that he called his home. The moment you relaxed your guard, the jackals made a meal of you.

Reina was nobody's meal, and when they came for him, they could expect to get their frigging teeth pushed down their throats. No matter who it was—Minelli, Aguirre, any of the others. He was not afraid of them. It was their place to be afraid, their place to watch their backs and hope he was not creeping up behind them in the dead of night. Or in broad daylight.

Ground floor, and one of Reina's hardmen stepped out of the elevator, looking both ways across the lobby like a scout preparing to convoy old ladies across the street. No sign of danger, and he gestured for the rest to follow, taking the point with one hand inside the open front of his suit coat.

Don Reina cleared the elevator, and the doors shut behind him. The gunners closed around him in a ring of flesh, preventing anyone from getting a clear view—or shot—at him. They walked in lock-step toward the tall revolving doors of the apartment house.

Outside, three Lincolns filled the curb as far as he could see through tinted doors and windows. Drivers standing by their cars, arms folded over jackets that concealed holstered hardware. Other gunmen at the head and tail of the stationary convoy, eyeing pedestrians and rooftops from behind dark glasses, suspecting everyone, trusting no one.

Another fifty feet and they were clear. Now almost to the doors, the sidewalk, Don Reina knew that he was being overcautious, even foolish.

Still...

The lead car suddenly disintegrated, swallowed by a burst of oily flame that raced along its length, consuming car and startled driver, hurling bits of twisted steel high into the air. The shock wave shattered tinted windows and revolving doors drove Don Reina and his storm troopers to the carpet, cringing from the rain of splintered glass.

The second car went up immediately, rising on its rear wheels like a stallion fighting its tether, riding a mushroom of flame that blackened the sidewalk and crisped the chauffeur where he had fallen after the initial blast. A scorching hell wind raced across the lobby of the windowless apartment house, fierce heat baking into Don Reina where he lay, beneath a burly bodyguard.

And number three exploded almost as an afterthought, the secondary detonation of its fuel tank spewing gasoline in all directions.

Giuseppe Reina felt the burning dampness, knew that he had wet himself. He looked at his trousers before he scrambled to his feet, and saw the evidence firsthand. His face was livid with embarrassment and anger as he called his troops together for the brisk march upstairs.

To change his pants.

Police would be arriving shortly and there would be the questions, endless questions that he would not answer even if he could.

And Don Reina had some searching questions of his own, that would be asked in private, away from the bright lights and snooping damned reporters. He would continue asking until he got the necessary information. Then...

There was a score to settle.

But first he had to make himself presentable, destroy the evidence of sudden, aching fear that gripped him like an icy hand.

He had to gird himself for war.

14

The delegates were in, except for Reina, who was clearly going to be late if he arrived at all. They had arrived throughout the morning and the early afternoon, parading past the burned-out hulks of limousines that had been moved but not concealed. In private, *capos* huddled with their underbosses and their *consiglieri*, checking rooms for listening devices, hidden cameras, ensuring that they were alone before they settled down to business.

They found no bugs, taps or cameras, perhaps because Minelli had not thought of it, perhaps because he still had faith in his own powers of persuasion. In any case, their talks were held in privacy before they ventured out to mingle with the others, renewing old friendships and making new acquaintances.

With the exception of New York's own bosses, most *capos* present did not know each other personally, and few had spoken on the phone, although their families may have been cooperating for generations in a wide variety of businesses. Telephones were unreliable, at best, and sheer attrition in the past few years had emptied local thrones as fast as they were occupied. Some regions had seen half a dozen dons within a year, as prosecution and assassination thinned the ranks, promoting those who otherwise would never have approached command rank in a lifetime.

Gradually the delegations came to know each other, forming cliques determined by geography, intermarriage, common interests. The largest and most secretive group included delegates from half a dozen jurisdictions drawn together by mutual distrust for Don Minelli.

The West Coast *capos*, Patriarcca and Cigliano, informally presided at the poolside gathering. Around them, slumped in deck chairs or reclining on chaise longues, alert despite appearances to the contrary, were Miami boss, Jerry Lazia, and two representatives of the New York families, Tom Gregorio and Frank Bonadonna. With their *consiglieri*, the group numbered nine, and they kept wary eyes on roving sentries whom Minelli had on duty around the grounds.

"Look at them now," Jules Patriarcca sneered. "Where were they when we needed them this morning?"

L.A. Lester took the cue. "That's right. We damn near get our asses fried in Ernie's own front yard, and where's his goddamn army, eh?"

The *capo* of Miami sipped his vodka Collins, cool eyes following the nearest sentry from behind his mirrored shades.

"You think it was a setup, then?" he asked.

"I couldn't tell you yes or no," Jules answered. "But I've got this feeling. Here." He rubbed his ample gut for emphasis.

"It don't make sense, Minelli tryin' to hit you here, when everybody else was due to show up any time."

"Who says it don't make sense?" Cigliano challenged. "Could be he wanted to be rid of us before you all got in."

"I'd say it was a sloppy job."

"You would, huh?"

Patriarcca raised a soothing hand. "Could be he didn't want to hit us, after all. It could have been a warning, like, to make us see things his way while we're on his turf."

Cigliano chimed in, adapting his tune to follow Patriarcca's lead.

"He's gonna need more votes than what he's got," the California *capo* said. "He wants to make it stick, he's gonna need a clear majority."

"We don't know what he wants yet."

"Bullshit."

"Lester—"

Tom Gregorio rocked forward on his chaise longue, motioning them all to silence.

"I know one thing," he informed them. "I got hit for half a mill today by some slick dude. The bastard laid a Black Ace on my banker up in Harlem, and the cretin let him have the whole day's take."

"An Ace?"

Patriarcca's voice was heavy with suspicion.

"That's what he said. No way to check it out, though."

"I hear Ernie's damn near got the Aces locked these days. You've seen the one he hangs around with? What's his name?"

"They call him Lazarus," Frank Bonadonna growled.

"Some say he's as good as Pat and Mike were in their prime," Gregorio put in.

"That right?"

"You think he put this thing together up in Harlem?"

Patriarcca spread his hands, frowning deeply. "I'm not saying that. There are Aces...and there are Aces. You follow?"

Gregorio looked puzzled, glancing from Patriarcca to Bonadonna, glowering in his confusion.

"That's right," Bonadonna put in. "Minelli's not the only one with Aces underneath his roof."

"But, say..." Gregorio was plainly loath to let go of a thought once he had finally come to grips with it. "Suppose the Aces were all getting back together, like the old days. Huh? If Ernie and this Lazarus could pull it all together..."

Lazia rattled the ice cubes in his glass.

"That takes a vote by the commission, Tom, remember?"

"Well..."

"It takes a vote if Ernie puts it to a vote," the *capo* of Seattle told them. "Now, if he should take it on himself to build a little private army out here in the country, quiet like...well, who's to know?"

"You think?"

"Goddamn it."

"Wait a sec', before you start to look for ghosts. Who says he's got an army, eh?"

"Why don't you look around here, Jerry?" L.A. Lester's voice was taut with anger. "All these suits ain't butlers, are they?"

"Whatsa matter, Les? You got no troops out on the coast?"

"I got enough. But I ain't got no friggin' Aces in the woodpile, that's for sure."

Frank Bonadonna cleared his throat, waiting until he had their full attention.

"Some smart-ass hit one of my powder factories earlier today," he said. "From what I put together so far, my man was a ringer for the one at Tommy's bank. I mean, he changes his clothes, but otherwise..."

"Uh-huh." The *capo* of Los Angeles sat back and rubbed his hands together, like a man who has just scored a telling point in some momentous argument.

"What's that supposed to mean?" Miami asked.

Gregorio jumped in.

"It means that everybody's getting hit around here, sudden like. Aguirre lost his downtown whorehouse. An' where the hell is Reina, anyway? I hear somebody bombed his place."

Lazia was chewing on his lower lip, deep in thought.

"You know," he said at last, "I *have* been getting rumbles down my way the past few weeks. Some kinda action with the Cubans and Colombians, like maybe someone's tryin' to go around behind my back, like, undercut my action.''

"There it is," Cigliano said, triumphant.

"There *what* is, for cryin' out loud?''

"Your proof, man.''

"Well, I don't—''

Jules Patriarcca's voice stilled them. "Let's all agree on this much, huh? Somebody has been taking liberties. We've all been touched. Somebody stands to gain if we lose out.''

"Damn right,'' Gregorio snapped.

"Okay. I say we wait and see what happens here today, tomorrow. If anybody tries to grab the whole pie for himself, I say we chop his fingers off an' teach the bastard a lesson.''

"I'll chop his fingers off, all right—at the goddamn throat,'' the California *capo* said.

A chorus of grumbled agreement ran around the circle, coming back to Patriarcca.

"Fine,'' he said at last. "We understand each other, then. No more, until we hear what Don Ernesto has to say.''

"Agreed.''

The little clique disintegrated, Lazia remaining poolside, while the rest retreated to their bungalows. Patriarcca walked slowly, L.A. Lester sticking to him like a shadow, counting Minelli's visible gunners for perhaps the hundredth time since they arrived.

It was an army of sorts. Enough to get the job done if Minelli should decide to round his guests up and dispose of them somewhere along the way. Perhaps, if the vote went against him...

Cigliano was saying something and Patriarcca shushed him, busy with his thoughts. His mind was occupied with the time zones now, and how long it would take to put another army in the air, to get it here in fighting form. A couple of hours, anyway, to gather in the troops and get them all aboard the plane. Another six or seven, minimum, to get them here.

They could be in by midnight if Patriarcca placed the call immediately.

They reached the adjoining bungalows and Patriarcca paused, turning to his shadow.

"I've got some calls to make now, Lester. I'd suggest you do the same."

It took an instant for the meaning to sink through, then Cigliano grinned.

"Hey, right. I get you. Sure. I'll call."

Jules nimbly retreated toward his cottage. He shook his head. The kid was damn near green as grass. It would be easy to reach out and pluck his territory like a ripe apple off the tree.

Later.

Right now the problem was survival, and Minelli was a green young punk, whatever might be said about his origins. He was a street-wise predator, and anyone who underestimated him could expect a grim surprise.

But Patriarcca had a few surprises of his own.

He let himself into the bungalow, frowning at the empty main room, lightening up as he heard woman sounds from the direction of the larger bedroom. It was a violation of tradition, bringing her along, but lately she had made Don Patriarcca feel so good, so young, he did not want to be without her. She was his lucky piece. His fountain of youth.

"Baby?"

She emerged from the bedroom, dressed in something frilly that he had not seen before. It instantly excited him, but Jules had other business on his mind right now.

"I gotta make a phone call, here," he told her, wondering why he felt this strange compulsion to explain himself. "I'll join you in a sec', and we can take a nap or somethin', 'kay?"

"You bet."

Her smile was hungry for him, and he felt the juices flowing, making him feel like a man. It had been years since Patriarcca had felt this way with any other woman, and he took it as an omen that his life was growing better, stronger, rather than declining with age.

The best years were ahead, and they could start tonight, if everything worked out as he had planned. If he could put an army in the field in time...

He dialed the long-distance operator, gave her the number in Seattle and told her to reverse the charges. No point in making Ernie cough up for the call that sealed his fate. Before the night was out he might be needing every dime he had to buy his life back.

Patriarcca waited through the rings until someone picked up the phone. He recognized the hard voice on the other end.

"Hey, Jimmy, this is me. That's right. I need some things."

And for the next ten minutes, Patriarcca told the listener of his needs, receiving an assurance that they would be met immediately. Finally satisfied, he cradled the receiver, already unbelting his robe as he moved toward the open bedroom door.

Time to feel young again.

Time for a booster shot of that magic she carried inside her.

And afterward, it would be time to meet with Don Minelli and the others. Time to be a statesman, then...and maybe, as the night wore on, there would be time for warriors, too.

15

Sally Palmer stood beneath the shower's stinging spray and let it cleanse her on the outside, slowly rinsing off the feel of hands. Her face upturned, eyes closed, she let the water pummel her across the neck and shoulders.

It would take more, she knew, to clean her on the inside, where it counted. Yes, a great deal more.

The lady Fed felt black and rotten inside, like a piece of fruit with insects working at the core. She knew it was irrational, ridiculous. She knew that she had only done her job. And yet...

She wondered if the taint showed through like crow's feet or a blemish on the skin. If so, Mack Bolan had not seemed to notice. Maybe she was learning how to hide it, maybe he had simply been hip deep in blood and rot too long to notice anything outside himself.

Sally hated herself for the thought and took another turn beneath the scalding shower to erase it from her mind. It was the shock of seeing him, and nothing else, which had revived those other memories of other times in the Manhattan hellgrounds. They had made a date back then, so many aching lives ago, but he had not been free to keep it, and she understood.

But still, it rankled.

She had been angry for a time. At Bolan. At herself, for being so irrational, for caring in a world where caring got you mangled, got you killed.

And she had missed him.

Damn it.

Sally turned the shower's single knob to cold. The driving, icy streams raised gooseflesh, and slowly rinsed away the dirty feeling.

It was work, and nothing more. Whatever Sally had to do in order to complete the job, it would be done. She had already bedded Patriarcca, and in time she might have to kill him.

Whatever was necessary, Sally Palmer knew that she was equal to the task.

But there was Bolan...

Stepping from the shower, reaching for a bath towel, Sally wondered what had brought him in on this one. He was unofficial now, she knew that much from rumors on the clandestine grapevine. Something had gone wrong, disastrously...and he was on the outside once more, looking in.

No, scratch that.

Bolan was a forward-looking soldier, Sally knew. If he was looking back at all, it was to watch his flank. And if he grieved at all, for anyone or anything, he did it on the inside, on his own time.

His presence here could only mean that there was something big at stake. The word about Eritrea had been a shocker, certainly, but Sally did not think a hostage would draw the Executioner across a continent to risk his life. Minelli's rumored coronation plans, now...that was something else again.

The Executioner's concern about Minelli was no less than that within the ranks, from what the lady Fed had so far overheard. She had been privy to the poolside conversation—she had had planted a miniature transmitter in the earpiece of Patriarcca's glasses one morning months ago when she had taken them "for repair"—and had listened in on his one-sided conversation with Seattle afterward. Within the hour, he would have an army airborne, headed eastward, and if she was not mistaken, others—Cigliano and Lazia, for openers—were likewise making preparations for a showdown.

She would have to reach Brognola and let him know what was about to happen. She still had time, and Jules was resting in the adjoining bedroom. He might desire her one more time before the sit-down, but she would be finished long before he found the strength to go again.

No point in even thinking of the telephone inside their bungalow. Jules might wake up at any time, surprise her, and she would be finished. Patriarcca cared for her, Sally knew, but only to a point. Where sex collided with his business world, emotion ended, cut off like a scream beneath the guillotine. He would destroy her instantly if he believed she had betrayed him, and Sally Palmer wanted better odds before she rolled the dice.

The house.

There would be telephones, of course, and perhaps a chance to use one unobserved. It was risky, but she had to take the chance.

Sally toweled herself dry, and donned a stylish jump suit, then carefully and soundlessly found her handbag and let herself out of the bungalow.

Dusk was perhaps an hour off. The coming darkness was an unknown quantity, and Sally wondered if the Executioner was traveling in it, bearing down upon her, on the enemy.

Angry at herself, she shook the moment off. She had a job to do. Never mind what Bolan might be thinking, doing, out there somewhere in the city. He was on a different track, pursuing different game, and if their paths should intersect, it would be chance, not fate, that made it happen.

From the side of her eye she noticed a gunner moving in a parallel course to hers toward the house. His stride was casual, unhurried, and she might have shrugged it off, except...

The lady Fed was no believer in coincidence. It was entirely possible that all things considered—an unfamiliar woman at a major sit-down, the morning's violence almost on his doorstep, the suspicion and distrust that hung over the compound like choking smog—Don Minelli had detailed a man to watch her.

It would be strange if he had *not* assigned a tail, she realized.

If it was a casual watch, he might not hang too close. She might evade his scrutiny if he was satisfied to know which room she occupied, for instance, rather than observing her firsthand at every moment. She might reach a telephone, if there was one inside a study, say, or...

She crossed the flagstone patio, conscious of the tail, and entered through a set of sliding glass doors into a sunken living room that could have easily contained a standard four-room tract house. Across the room, three gunners lounged on chairs and sofas, talking among themselves.

She heard the tail come in behind her.

Sally traveled on her instincts, seeking out the kitchen first to give her visit the appearance of a logical motive. If nothing else, she hoped that she could duck her shadow there and find a telephone without him hanging on behind her.

The kitchen was restaurant size. Half a dozen workers dressed in spotless whites were already well into the dinner preparations. Sally smelled roast beef, spaghetti, sauces that she could not identify offhand. A youngish woman in a maid's costume brushed past and Sally buttonholed her, got directions to the washroom.

Her tail was with her as she left the kitchen, hanging back but making no attempt to mask his mission as he followed her along a well-lighted corridor with doors on either side. Sally reached her destination, ducked inside and closed the door without a backward glance.

Befitting Don Minelli's style, the washroom was equipped with plush velvet sofas, a wall-length mirror—and a telephone.

The lady Fed wondered briefly what might have possessed the man to put one here, decided finally that his sense of propriety tended toward extravagance at every level. Still, she did not plan to look a gift horse in the mouth.

She lifted the receiver, marginally encouraged by the humming of the dial tone, wondering if there was any code required to reach an outside line. No time to worry now, and with her eyes fixed on the door, she swiftly dialed Brognola's office number, waiting through the rings until his private secretary picked it up.

"Hello?"

"It's Flasher. Is my uncle in?"

"I'm sorry, no. He's in New York."

Sally's heart leaped into her throat.

"Is there a local number I can call?"

The secretary stalled, put off by Sally's flagrant breach of regular procedures. When she finally answered, there was caution in her voice.

"Again, who is this, please?"

"It's Flasher," she repeated, reining in her temper with an effort. "And it's top priority."

"I see."

Another pause, with the background noise of fingers riffling through a Rollodex. It seemed to take forever for the secretary to respond.

"I have the hotel's number. It's the best I can do."

"That's fine," Sally replied, committing it to memory, repeating it for confirmation.

"If he calls..."

Sally thought about it, frowned.

"There isn't any message. If I can't get through at this end, I'll take care of it myself."

"I beg your pardon?"

Tall, dark and attractive, the leader closed the gap with easy strides. His flanker was a classic button man, devoid of all originality.

"A word, if you don't mind, about your phone call."

Sally arched an eyebrow, striving for the sort of arrogance Mob courtesans reserve for underlings.

"And if I *do* mind?"

"I'm afraid I must insist."

A finger snap, and suddenly her shadow was beside her, taking her by the arm and steering her along the corridor. She tried to pull away, and then the button had her other arm, his fingers digging in like talons, hurting her deliberately.

Her mind was racing as they trailed the tall man along the hall, toward the center of the house. Unbidden, Bolan flashed across her thoughts and then was gone, replaced by brooding dread.

She was in trouble, and she knew it.

16

David Eritrea shifted on the metal cot, searching in vain for a comfortable position. The lumpy slab of mattress was bad enough, but he was further limited in movements by the handcuffs that secured his left wrist to one leg of the cot, which in turn had been securely bolted to the floor.

He knew he wasn't going anywhere until Minelli thought the time was right. The disposition of his case was preordained, of course. He had informed, and never mind the reasons that had guided his decision. The penalty for violation of *omerta*'s silent code was death. The only question left concerned the time and method of his execution.

Minelli had some use for him; that much was clear. The hit team could have killed him in his home with far less effort than they spent abducting him, his wife...

The thought of Sarah, never far from him through the past three days, made Eritrea sick at heart. Minelli could not let her live, not now, and for Eritrea, there was no way to skirt the guilt that came with knowing she faced death because of him.

She might be dead already, and for a stomach-churning moment, he almost hoped it was true. If they were in a hurry, they would not have the time for...other things.

Eritrea had seen and done enough himself to know what might befall his wife in hostile hands. He blocked the grisly images with force of will alone, and concentrated on the question of his own continuing survival.

In the federal witness program, cut off from the day-to-day intrigue of Mafia life, he had lost track of the contenders for old Augie Marinello's empty throne. Minelli was a fleeting memory, a lowly troop commander at the time Eritrea made his power play and ran headlong into the Bolan juggernaut.

Mack Bolan.

Dave Eritrea could never hear the name without a flood of mixed emotions. Bolan had destroyed his dreams of empire, boundless power, forced him into exile, in the company of strangers. And yet...

At another level, almost subconsciously, Eritrea retained a grudging admiration for the soldier who had brought him down. The guy had guts and style, no doubt about it. He had suckered everyone, the whole five families, and had them dancing to his tune as neat as you please. Nobody else had come as close to standing the brotherhood on its ear.

He almost wished that Bolan was around today, to shake things up...and maybe take Eritrea the hell away from there. It would have been a handy out, but David knew the hellfire guy was dead.

It had been a jolt, those newspaper headlines, laying down how Bolan had flamed out in Central Park. Right there on Eritrea's own home ground, but too damned late to do the former mafioso any good. The stud had pushed his luck too far, misjudged the opposition, and his time ran out. Spectacularly.

The bastard even died with style.

And at the same time, Dave Eritrea had felt a twinge of sadness at the soldier's passing. Not that they were friends or anything, far from it. In his day, Eritrea would have gladly gouged the warrior's eyes out with his fingers, given half a chance.

But you had to have respect for someone who retained his sense of honor to the bitter end and never gave an inch. He lived and died by the vendetta, sure, and that was something any mafioso could relate to. The blood debt, sometimes spanning generations, aching to be paid in still more blood.

Eritrea had no idea precisely what had put Bolan on the Mafia's case. It was so long ago, the stories handed down by word of mouth so jumbled and distorted. No one who had been there when it started was alive today, as far as he could tell, and in the end, it hadn't mattered how the war began so much as how it seemed about to end. Bolan moved too fast and hit too hard for anyone to waste time studying his goddamned roots.

But that was over now. The soldier had flamed out, and there Eritrea sat, with one wrist handcuffed to a metal cot. Waiting to die.

As if in answer to his thoughts came the sound of heavy footsteps in the corridor outside. Then someone fumbled with the lock, and the door was opened briefly and as quickly closed.

Minelli stood beyond Eritrea's reach, regarding him with an expression that was composed equally of loathing and concern.

The loathing he might feel for any turncoat who informed against the brotherhood.

The concern was in case Eritrea should cheat him, foil his plans by dying sooner than desired.

"You really ought to eat," Minelli said.

"I haven't had much appetite."

"I understand. It's safe, you know. I don't intend to poison you."

Eritrea smiled, surprised at how easy it came. "Just trying to fatten up the turkey, huh?"

Minelli's shrug conveyed supreme indifference. "It's up to you. Tonight we finish it, regardless."

Just like that. Eritrea felt his stomach churning.

"So. You finally found your nerve," he said.

The laughter chilled Eritrea.

"That's good. I hoped you'd be a man about it."

"That'll be one man between us."

Laughter died, but Don Minelli's face remained serene.

"You can't provoke me, David. Sorry. I need you. Just until tonight. You're my ace in the hole."

Eritrea frowned. He had no feel for what was coming, just a vague and growing sense of apprehension.

"I don't follow you."

Minelli raised an eyebrow, frowned.

"Of course not. And why should you? I keep forgetting that you've...been away."

Minelli started pacing, careful to remain outside the radius of Dave Eritrea's grasp.

"No reason why you shouldn't know." His captor paused, almost dramatically, for maximum effect. "You're going to my coronation, David. Not exactly guest of honor...no, I'd say you fall more in the line of entertainment."

Bits and pieces of the puzzle came together in Eritrea's mind. He knew Minelli was ambitious, but...the boss of bosses? That would take some doing. A gift to *la commissione*, perhaps—like Dave Eritrea's head—but even then...

Eritrea knew there must be more.

"A present doesn't make a coronation," he informed Minelli.

"Ah, but that depends on who delivers it. I haven't just got you. I've got the blood right, David."

Eritrea frowned. "Minelli? I don't—"

His captor interrupted him.

"The name is Marinello, David."

And Eritrea could not head off astonishment before it reached his face. Minelli's words had struck him like a fist above the heart.

"You understand now."

"Anyone can claim—"

"Enough!"

The eyes of the man he knew as Minelli were flashing at him, color rising in the swarthy cheeks. For just an instant, he was ready to attack, to step within Eritrea's reach, but then the mafioso caught himself and prudently stood clear.

"Everyone believed my father childless...and he was, from all appearances. His wife was barren, but he craved an heir. A man of his virility..."

Minelli hesitated, wrestling with private feelings for a moment, finally continuing.

"My mother bore two children for him. One, a girl, was stillborn. I survived. The church forbids divorce, and there were still appearances to be maintained. I never met my father formally. Barney Matilda made all the arrangements for our home, the schools."

It made a crazy kind of sense to Dave Eritrea now. Matilda, unacknowledged father of the deadly Taliferro twins, had long experience hiding secrets of his own. And Augie...

"He was bringing me along, inside the family, and teaching me the ropes. In time, I would have been the old man's *consiglieri*, or an underboss, in line to claim his chair on *la commissione*. When Bolan took him out..."

The words trailed off and Dave Eritrea could see it now. The young man waiting to fill his father's shoes someday. Except the shoes and legs and all were blown away in Jersey, after Marinello Senior lost round one to Mack the bastard, way back when. Round two came down in Pittsfield, and there hadn't been enough of Augie left to bury in a sandwich bag.

The sudden topside vacancy had caused a scramble for succession, with Minelli still too far removed from power to have a decent shot. Eritrea himself had won the toss, and others had succeeded him in turn, as Bolan, Mother Nature and the federal strike force whittled down the ranks.

But it was time for new blood. Minelli had the Marinello family in his pocket as it was, and with a little push the throne was well within his reach.

"You'll still need proof," Eritrea said, aware that it had sounded lame, that someone with Minelli's acumen would have it covered half a dozen different ways.

"I have my father's letters, some from Barney to my mother. And the old man's wife...she kept a diary. Seems she knew about us all along, and just kept quiet."

Dave Eritrea could think of nothing more to say. Minelli had it covered, and short of insurrection in the ranks, he probably could pull it off.

Capo di tutti capi. The boss of bosses.

"You need your rest," Minelli said. "I have enjoyed our little chat. I'll send somebody for you in a little while."

Minelli's hand was on the doorknob when Eritrea's voice arrested him.

"My wife."

The *capo* turned, a shadow flickering across his face and momentarily edging out the quiet triumph there.

"Forget about her, David. You've got grief enough right here."

And he was gone, but there was something—in his eyes, his tone—that set Eritrea thinking.

Something had gone wrong, perhaps. If Sarah had escaped, somehow, she might...

The hostage closed that door inside his mind and locked it, threw away the key. There would be no escaping from the gun crew Don Minelli set to watch her. Sarah would be dead by now, or worse, and there was nothing in the world that he could do to help her.

Don Minelli.

Make that Don Marinello.

And the sound of the name was enough to take Eritrea back a dozen years and more. It was like stepping through a time warp. A crushing sense of déjà vu had settled in around his shoulders like a grim, oppressive weight.

It was ironic, after all the waiting, scheming and killing he had done to seize the former Marinello throne and claim

it for his own, that Dave Eritrea would be involuntarily instrumental in bringing yet another Marinello back to power
in New York and nationwide.

Ironic.

And bitter to the core.

The former mafioso thought of Sarah once again. And
wept.

"IT WOULD BE SO MUCH EASIER if you'd just tell us
everything."

The lady Fed regarded her interrogator with disdain.

"I've done that. Twice." She tried a different tack. "I
don't think Jules is going to like this game, do you?"

"Which game is that?" the tall man asked.

"This twenty-questions nonsense. He'll be waiting for
me. And he doesn't like to be kept waiting."

"Ah. Well, I believe that in the circumstances, Mr. Patriarcca would be sympathetic to our curiosity. He's quite a
cautious man himself."

"This is ridiculous."

He sat down opposite Sally, chair and body blocking access to the study door.

"Let's try it one more time," he said, his face deadpan.
"From the beginning. Why didn't you use the phone inside
your cottage?"

Sally heaved a tired, exaggerated sigh.

"I didn't want to wake Jules up. He was...resting."

She put enough of the suggestive innuendo in her voice to
let the soldier know precisely what had tired Jules out.
Enough to let him know that he could have the same, if it
would get her off the hook.

He passed.

"I see. And so, you made your call—long distance—from
the washroom."

She spread her open hands. "You don't want people using it, why don't you take the damned thing out?"

"You called your...uncle...was it?"

"That's right. Why don't you check it with your second set of ears?"

"The name is Lazarus," he told her, frost behind the words. "And it's been checked."

"Well, then..."

"And you identified yourself as Flasher, I believe. A family nickname, wasn't it?"

Another weary sigh, to mask the rising apprehension.

"My uncle made a joke one time, about some of my baby pictures. I was naked."

No suggestive undertone this time. The man called Lazarus was obviously immune.

"Your uncle's name and address, please."

"Get screwed. You think I'm dragging family into your dream world, you're worse off than I thought."

He stiffened, coloring, but held himself in check.

"What was the purpose of your call?"

"I told you twice. His wife—my aunt—has got a birthday coming up. I wanted some suggestions on a gift."

The hardman fished inside his outer jacket pocket, produced a compact tape recorder that he placed between them on the coffee table. One long index finger found the button, brought the little deck to life, his eyes never leaving Sally's face.

"There isn't any message. If I can't get through at this end, I'll take care of it myself."

And click. The tape went dead.

"What is it you were planning to take care of, then? A birthday gift?"

"That's right. You never heard of birthday presents?"

"Oh, I've heard of many things. Spies, for instance. Always sticking snotty noses into other people's business, till they get chopped off."

"What's that got to do with me?"

It was the hardman's turn to sigh. The tape deck disappeared inside his pocket and he rose to stand above her.

"I was hoping you'd cooperate," he told her earnestly. "I see that won't be possible. It will be necessary to persuade you."

Sally felt a chill run down her spine.

"Now wait a second, buster—"

"No more time for waiting. You will tell me what I need to know. Tonight, perhaps tomorrow."

The lady Fed was on her feet but going nowhere.

"Jules—"

"Will understand completely, I assure you. And if not..."

He left the statement hanging there, unfinished, telling Sally everything she had to know about his status in the scheme of things. If he was big enough to call the tune for Patriarcca...

Sally didn't want to think about that. Her mind was on the problem of survival, and she could not see beyond the next few moments. There was pain in store, she knew that much, and wondered how long she could keep the secrets locked inside before she broke, spilled everything.

An hour? Two?

There had been briefings, lectures, on the possibility of capture and interrogation, but reality was something else again. Her flesh was crawling as she waited, mind alert and seeking an escape hatch, finding none.

She was trapped, and there was no way out, no way to reach the other side of it, without proceeding head-on through the middle. Through the pain.

And Sally passed beyond the question of remaining silent, no longer wondering how long she could last.

She wondered now if she would live.

If she could cling to life, at least.

If she would wish to.

17

The phone rang twice before Brognola's gruff, familiar voice came on the line.

"Hello?"

"LaMancha. Can you talk?"

"It's clear."

Outside the service-station phone booth, traffic flowed along Franklin D. Roosevelt Drive. Bolan had a view of the Williamsburg Bridge, the flat sheen of the East River in the middle distance.

"I'm running out of numbers," he informed the Fed. "If Don Minelli has Eritrea, he's in the compound now."

"So's Flasher," Hal reminded him unnecessarily.

"I know."

Brognola's voice was hesitant and edged with apprehension when he spoke. "It could be that we've got a problem there."

An arctic tremor ran down Bolan's spine. "Explain."

"My office got a call from Flasher, two, three hours back. She got my number here, but there's been nothing since. No message, *nada*."

Bolan read the worry in his old friend's tone.

"You figure she's been made?"

"It's possible. The phone was risky. Then again..."

He did not have to sketch the various alternatives for Bolan. Sally might have lost her access to the telephone for any one of several reasons. There was no good reason to believe her cover had been blown, and yet...

The soldier's primal instincts spoke to him, alerting him to danger. If she had been overheard, somehow...

If Patriarcca or Minelli were aware of Sally's double role...

If they were working on her, even now...

Goddamn it, *if!*

He refused to follow the morbid train of thought where it led. The Executioner had been that way before and required no grim reminders of the scenery.

"I'm going in tonight," he told Brognola. "Any sooner would be self-defeating."

"Yeah. You know, I've just been thinking maybe I should drop in on Minelli. Sort of crash the party, see what's up."

"Without a stack of warrants? You'd have lawyers coming out your ears, guy. It could mean your job."

"Job, hell, they'd have my ass for breakfast," Hal retorted. "Funny thing is, none of that seems too important at the moment."

Bolan heard his old friend's pain and shared it. The hurting fear that comes with knowing someone dear has laid it on the line and may have lost it all. The empty pain that rides ahead of knowing, one way or the other.

"Don't blow it," Bolan cautioned him. "What's done is done...and, anyway, for all we know, she's fine."

"I guess."

Brognola didn't sound convinced.

"And if she's...damaged...well, there's only so much you can do to make it right."

A long silence on Brognola's end, eventually broken by a weary sigh.

"I heard from Sticker, indirectly," Hal said, glad to change the subject. "Everybody's in, as far as we can tell."

"Vibrations?"

"Cautious. Edgy. Maybe hostile. Everybody's stewing."

Bolan felt glad that his blitz was having the desired effect upon his enemies.

"I'll let it simmer until dark," he said. "I should be in before they're ready for the main event."

"I could arrange to have some people in the neighborhood," Brognola offered.

"Up to you. Make sure you've got a net before you start to saw the limb off, eh?"

The man from Justice snorted.

"You're the one to talk. Say, listen...on this other thing..."

"I'll bring them with me if I can," the soldier told him.

"Hell, I know that. Don't you think I know that?" Hal's distress was coming through as irritation now. "But if you can't...I mean, it doesn't have a thing to do with you."

The warrior's frown was carved in stone.

"It has to do with all of us," he answered grimly.

Silence.

Then Brognola said, "I guess it does."

The Executioner prepared to disengage.

"I've got some other calls to make before I move," he told his friend. "Do what you have to do."

"I'll see you, huh?"

"I wouldn't be surprised."

The dial tone filled his ear, and Bolan eased the telephone receiver back into its cradle, fishing in his pocket for another coin. He concentrated on his mission, the preparations for his coming strike, but there was no way to evade the nagging dread that came with Hal Brognola's message.

Bolan knew the odds too well to cherish hope. If Sally had not been discovered, she was still in mortal danger, more so as the time slipped past, the numbers counting down to zero hour.

For the moment, he was certain only that she was in there, somewhere, and in peril. Trapped inside the dragon's lair, with Dave Eritrea, with Sticker—all of them within his field of fire, precise locations unknown until he was inside.

Until it was too late.

But he had other calls to make before the doomsday clock ran down, and he was out of numbers. The Executioner could not afford a tardy entrance to Minelli's coronation, any more than he could be late to his own damn funeral.

And Bolan knew the two events might well turn out to be one and the same.

BROGNOLA HELD THE CARTRIDGES IN ONE HAND, rattling them absentmindedly, his thoughts a world away. His .38 revolver, open, empty, filled his other fist. The bedside telephone rebuked him with its stony silence.

"Dammit."

And he knew he should be doing *something*, but the specifics of the thing eluded him.

It should have been a simple job for Flasher, in and out, disguised as Patriarcca's window dressing, with a full report through channels when she had the time. From all appearances, she had discovered something that refused to wait, its urgency compelling her to risk her cover—and her life—to get a message out.

And he had missed her, for the sake of being in New York and closer to the action.

"Dammit!"

It had been a simple in and out, except that somehow everything had suddenly become balled up along the way. Eritrea had disappeared from what had passed for a safehouse and the Executioner arrived to track him down and bring him back, alive or otherwise. Tattaglia was in the middle of it and heading up the Maryland contingent at the sit-down, likely to be caught in the Minelli-Bolan crossfire when it broke. And when it broke, there would be no safe havens in the hellgrounds, not for friend or foe.

But it was Flasher who preyed on Hal Brognola's mind the most. He felt responsible—all right, he *was* responsible, goddamn it—for the danger she was in. He called the shots, he chose the jobs, and in the end if things went sour, he would have to bear the heat.

Except that he would be sitting in his hotel room, safe and sound, while agents in the field were dying.

"If she's damaged, there's only so much you can do to make it right."

Bolan's words came back to him and he was right, of course. Brognola's temperament and years of going at least loosely by the book prevented him from pulling out the stops and wreaking vengeance on the animals he tracked from day to day. He could investigate them to his heart's content and bust them if he found them dirty. He could kill them, on occasion, if they tried to kill him first, although he never really got the feel for it. And where was Justice, really, once the lawyers with their Latin phrases and the judges in their funeral robes were done?

"There's only so much you can do..."

But there were no such limitations on the Executioner. His options were wide open, and he was free to make the penalty approximate the crime.

"To make it right."

Some things could never be made right, of course. Some crimes could only be avenged, and with a fury that eclipsed the savage act itself. Some human animals could only understand apocalyptic retribution for their crimes against humanity.

More than once, Brognola had observed the Executioner in frenzy mode, imposing his revenge on the cannibals, and the images were branded on his soul. Miami. Boston. Jersey and Detroit. The blood-and-thunder aftermath of his betrayal in Virginia, April Rose's death.

The soldier, with an infinite capcity for caring, seemed to have an infinite capacity for killing, too. And if Minelli had discovered Flasher, if his men had harmed Sally in any way...

Brognola grimaced.

He would not have traded places with the mafioso at any price.

While Bolan lived, Minelli would not find a hiding place on earth. No mountaintop, no cave, no desert island would be wild enough, remote enough, to shelter him from the avenging spirit. No matter where he ran, he would be hunted down precisely like the vermin that he was, and run to earth. Wiped out.

But the big Fed knew from watching Bolan at work that vengeance never filled the void of martyred friends and lost loved ones. Retribution was a form of hellfire therapy, of repaying a debt in blood and purging grief, but ultimately it added nothing to the man or to society beyond elimination of a hostile predator. When it was done, the ritual complete, a legacy of grief remained, and there was nothing more to do but live with it.

Mack Bolan had eradicated countless savages—one unofficial tabulation placed it in the thousands—and he bore the scars of losses that had cut him to the soul and left it bleeding, raw. Remembered pain was never far away, Brognola knew, and each new skirmish seemed to add another scar.

He wondered, sometimes, how the Executioner held on. How long could he keep going, butting heads against the odds, against his own mortality?

One more time, he thought, not realizing that it sounded like a prayer. This time, at least.

For Flasher.

For Tattaglia.

And for the man himself.

They could not well afford to lose him now, could not afford to let him lose himself. It was incredible that Bolan had maintained his balance as it was, an exile, every hand against him.

How many other men had cracked beneath the strain of lesser weights? How many had withdrawn into themselves or detonated into wild, chaotic violence aimed at members of their families, at total strangers, when the fuse burned down too far?

Mack Bolan was a living mystery. A goddamned wonder of the world. No other like him had arisen during living memory; there might not be another like him in a lifetime.

And they needed him. Alive. In working order and in fighting trim.

Brognola's job, on paper, was to make sure that Bolan did not run amok, initiate another of his one-man wars. He had accepted the assignment knowing that it was impossible, that no one would contain the hellfire warrior's energy until he was nailed inside a stout pine box.

The misconception had been in the assumption that Bolan would be "starting something" once his last official ties were severed. Nothing, Hal Brognola knew, could have been farther from the truth.

The Executioner had never started anything, and he was not about to try. His war had been there waiting for him when he came home from the Asian hellgrounds all those lives ago, and he had been fighting it ever since. There was no new war for Mack Bolan. It would always be the same old war, despite the shifting battlefields, the changing names and faces of his enemies.

The opposition was—had always been, would always be—the savages who prey upon society.

The warrior's sole objective was—had always been, would always be—to drive them back into their caves and keep them there, to make them fear the cleansing light of day.

And Bolan was—had always been, would always be—the Executioner.

Damn straight.

It was Mack Bolan's war, but there was room for allies, so long as they did not obstruct the field of fire. If there was nothing Hal could do to rein the hellfire warrior in—or, God forbid, to call him off—there might be something he could do to help.

Brognola finished loading his revolver, holstered it and reached for the telephone.

18

Bill Rafferty was beside the phone when it rang. With some sixth sense that develops in a lawman over time, he had been expecting the call. As he lifted the receiver, he already knew who was on the other end.

"Rafferty."

"How's your houseguest?"

Bolan's casual tone surprised the veteran detective, and the short hairs on his neck stood at attention.

"She's in safe hands," the strike-force chief replied. "Your friend in Washington sent out a pickup team."

"I see."

He heard the concern in Bolan's voice.

"I checked their paperwork, of course. They were legit, for what it's worth."

"It's worth a lot. And thanks."

"Don't mention it."

"Have you made a decision, Captain?"

Cool and casual. He might have been requesting tomorrow's weather forecast rather than inviting Rafferty to join in mortal combat.

"Yeah, I have." The gruff detective glanced around him, hesitating for another moment, finally releasing held-in breath. "I guess I'll go along."

Just that. And Rafferty was perfectly aware that he had sealed his fate with five small words. If anything went wrong from here on in, it was his ass, his job, his pension on the line.

"Okay." There was a mixture of relief and sadness in the soldier's tone. "You know Minelli's place?"

"Out on the island? Yeah."

"His visitors are in for a surprise tonight, at...let's say...1900."

"Couldn't happen to a nicer crowd."

And he could almost *hear* Bolan grin across the wires.

"Our mutual acquaintance has a friend inside, with the Seattle delegation. The rumble is, she may be made."

"Bad luck."

"There's more. Minelli has your missing package under wraps."

If figured, sure.

"Sounds like a tricky play," said Rafferty.

"They may be still intact. But either way, the party goes."

It came out cold, but Rafferty could sense a certain pain behind the words. And he was learning more about Bolan by the moment.

"So what's my end?"

"You're batting cleanup. There should be a lot of strays, and some of them may be inclined to talk, if you're persuasive."

"I'm a charmer when I need to be."

"Okay. I'll rig it so you get a tip in time to roll and make it look legitimate. If everything comes off, you should be covered five by five. Stay hard, Captain."

"Yeah. You, too."

He thought of something else and snatched the telephone receiver back, but he was talking to the dial tone now. The Executioner was gone.

And what else do you tell a man whose life is on the line around the clock, by choice? What do you say before the solitary soldier goes to war?

Be careful?

Keep your head down?

Hit the bastards once for me?

It was simple, really. There was nothing to be said.

The soldier's actions would be speaking for him soon.

And whichever way it went, Bill Rafferty would be on Bolan's flank tonight, ready to receive the stragglers as they fled the firestorm.

Rafferty was well aware that he'd be violating every code of conduct in the book, that he could lose his job, his freedom, if the truth came out in open court. But somehow the veteran detective's own priorities were shifting, changing, to accommodate a different set of values, different than but not entirely foreign to his own.

Bill Rafferty had seen too many criminals sheltered while their victims were crucified. He was familiar with the lawyers on both sides—the prosecution and defense—who jumped at sweetheart deals to clear the calendar, without regard for morality. He had seen hundreds of convicted felons walk away with reprimands, and fines that scarcely dented their illicit bankrolls.

He had seen enough to know the hallowed system wasn't working anymore. Perhaps it never had, but there was nothing he could do to change the past.

There might be something, though, that he could do about the present...and the future. Anyway, the strike-force captain felt compelled to try. And if he lost it all in the attempt...

Well, it was better than surrendering without a fight.

And when Bill Rafferty went out, he meant to go out fighting, taking down as many hostiles as he could along the way.

It was the only decent way, he thought, for any fighting man to go.

MACK BOLAN HAD AN HOUR to prepare himself for Don Minelli's sit-down, and the time weighed heavily on him as he pushed the rental wheels eastbound along Highway 25A, crossing out of Nassau County and into Long Island proper.

He knew how long an hour was and what could happen in that time.

He knew what could become of Sally Palmer and Dave Eritrea if Minelli tried to start his party prematurely, using one or both of them to enliven the festivities.

Eritrea was certain to be marked for death, presumably when all the *capos* were assembled, so that they could marvel at Minelli's cunning, his ability to reach inside the federal witness program and extract so ripe a plum. As for Sally, there was a chance that she had not yet been made.

The soldier's memory coughed up unbidden images of other comrades, other loved ones, mangled in the grim machinery of Bolan's everlasting war. Some had been agents, others innocent civilians caught up at the wrong place, the wrong time, paying with their lives for an association with the Executioner.

He tried to close the door on painful memories, but they were flooding back, full force now. Helpless "turkeys," butchered by the Mafia for information or perhaps to serve as grisly object lessons for the brotherhood.

Bolan shook the thoughts away. He had no time for ghosts. The friendly spirits would be with him when he needed them. As for the hostiles, well, there were fresh ones at his target destination, waiting to be made.

But he could not ignore the danger Sally Palmer faced there, inside the serpent's den.

The Executioner was not responsible for Sally's presence in the hostile camp, but he would bear the weight of full responsibility for what went down inside those walls tonight.

Never for an instant did the soldier contemplate a deviation from his plan. The course was set and he would see it through, to victory or death, but still, he could not hide the concern he felt for some of those inside.

The lady Fed would live or she would die. The risks had been no secret going in.

And if she lost it at Minelli's, Bolan would do everything within his power to even up the score. If Sally had been...damaged...it would be scorched earth for Don Ernesto and his company. A firestorm that would make New York sit up and pay attention—for perhaps a day or so.

The city was unfeeling, cold, and there was a monotony about its crime reports—on the rapes, muggings, murders, maimings—that suggested its denizens learned nothing from their mistakes. As each new wave of outrage passed, succeeded by a swell of apathy, the same old attitudes returned, defying predators at large to offer yet more shocking entertainment on the late-night news.

The city bred indifference, a bland disdain for humankind that Bolan found contemptuous in itself. A city boy, he had been raised to know his neighbors, care about their problems, sympathize—and help, if possible. Apathy was abhorrent to him just as disease, starvation and oppression were abhorrent. Indifference was stagnation to the Executioner, indifference was a synonym for living death.

And Bolan *was* involved up to his eyebrows in the fight to help his fellow man. The soldier long ago had recognized and reconciled himself to the demanding role of his brother's keeper. He could not bc everywhere, help everyone, but where he was, he left a mark.

And at the moment, he was in New York.

He had already left his mark upon the Mafia families who had raped the city for so long. They knew him well, and they would know him better before this night was done.

One man *could* make a difference, with determination, courage, will.

One man *could* help another, even over protest, if he went that extra mile and risked it all.

One man like Bolan.

And Sally Palmer had learned that lesson well. She was striking blows against the common enemy before she met the Executioner, and there was still a chance...

The Executioner concentrated on the last few miles of highway, pushing it to give himself some extra on-site preparation time. He would need every moment of it before he crashed Minelli's coronation party. And he had a few unscheduled party favors for the honored guests from out of town. The life of the party was coming.

The death of the party was here.

With any luck at all, he would bring the house down. Square on Don Ernesto's head.

19

The woman's eyes were red from crying, and the left one was already swelling shut. Mascara tracked down her bruised cheeks. Her lower lip was split and bleeding freely, crimson droplets soaking through the blouse above one breast.

Ernesto Minelli shook his head and frowned, a parody of sympathy. His eyes were as cold as slate when he turned back to face the man called Lazarus.

"And nothing?"

"Give it time. She's obviously field conditioned, but she'll break. They always break."

The Ace's smile reminded Minelli of a hungry reptile.

"We haven't got the time. If Patriarcca thinks that he can fuck around with me—"

"She doesn't work for Jules."

The bland pronouncement startled Minelli into momentary silence, and he took another long look at the battered lady, bound securely to the wooden chair in front of them. The implication of Lazarus's words took time to register.

"Well, who then? What the hell...?"

"Who do you know in Washington?"

"In Washington?" The *capo*'s mind went momentarily blank, and he was locked in on a mental image of Seattle. "But you just said—"

"In Washington, D.C."

Minelli didn't like the patronizing tone that Lazarus adopted, but he let it pass, already grasping what the Ace was getting at.

"The Feds?"

"I'd bet my life on it."

"You do that," Minelli growled, recovering, enjoying the suggestion of a flush on the other man's face. "You do exactly that. And if you're wrong, if this one doesn't talk..."

"She'll talk. No sweat."

"No sweat, my ass. If this thing falls apart, we all go down, your precious Aces, everything."

"I'm well aware..."

"I hope so," Minelli snapped, not giving Lazarus the time to finish it. "I hope you're well aware that your head's on the block, right there alongside mine."

"That's understood."

"So do your job and get it over with. Before the meeting breaks downstairs, I wanna know the who and why and all of it. I wanna know what this one had for breakfast on her fourteenth birthday. You got it?"

Lazarus regarded him from under hooded eyelids for a moment, nodding slowly.

"Done."

Then the *capo* left, relaxing slightly when the study door had closed behind him, cutting off the reptile stare. He made a conscious effort to unwind as he paced down the corridor of the meeting hall.

They would be gathering to hear him soon, to listen with their varying degrees of loyalty or suspicion, thinly veiled hostility or cool respect. It was a loaded audience, he knew, but Minelli felt a power growing within him now, the strength that was his birthright flowing electrically in his blood.

He could do anything tonight, and screw the Feds if they had any thoughts of pulling the net around him now, when he was so damned close to having everything. They were too late, and knowing that increased the bounce in his stride.

So what if Patriarcca's bitch was working for the government? She had attempted one phone call since her arrival, and had failed to make connections then. She left no message for her boss—whoever he might be—and any information she had passed along before arriving in New York would deal with Jules and no one else.

If anyone was on the hook, therefore, it would be Patriarcca, and that suited Minelli fine.

A federal prosecution might remove him from the scene and make room for a more deserving candidate.

Like Lazarus, perhaps.

The Ace was getting too damned big for Minelli's liking, and his attitude was verging on insubordination. When everything was settled at the conference, there would have to be some changes in the *capo*'s own security machine, and there should be no problem in finding someone capable of taking up the slack once Lazarus was gone.

The Aces, after all, were known as much for their adaptability as for their grim ferocity in punishing La Cosa Nostra's enemies.

That settled, Minelli allowed himself a smile, the first sincere one of the day. His morning had begun with grim foreboding, but the night was proving to be another game entirely. Everything was coming off as planned, and just a few more hours would confirm his grip upon the reins of power in the brotherhood.

The boss of bosses. *Capo di tutti capi.*

The hungry smiles became a booming laugh, which carried Minelli on toward the meeting hall and destiny.

THE EXECUTIONER WAS RIGGED FOR DOOMSDAY in the dark. The hidden pockets of his blacksuit were filled with the grim machinery of silent death. His hands and face were camouflaged with jungle war paint, making sure that nothing brighter than his eyes would catch a moonbeam and betray his presence on the grounds before he meant to make it known.

Big Thunder, the .44 AutoMag, rode his hip on military webbing, and the sleek Beretta nestled underneath his arm. Extra magazines for both the side arms circled Bolan's waist, the pouches interspersed with smoke and frag grenades arranged for quick retrieval. Other bandoliers of ammunition and explosives looped across his chest and further weighed the warrior down.

Bolan's main weapon for the strike was an Uzi submachine gun, selected for its convenience and firepower. Just under eighteen inches overall, with folding stock collapsed, the little stutter gun's effective killing range of one hundred yards would easily exceed the soldier's needs this time around.

When the killing started, Bolan would be thrown to center stage of what was shaping up as the most concentrated gathering of mafiosi since Miami, early in his private war. He wanted there to be no doubt of where he was and what was happening. It was another bloody generation's turn to live—and die—with terror, as countless of their victims had been doing since the Executioner's own "second mile" against the Mob.

They had grown soft, complacent, cocky in his absence, and the warrior was ready to begin his purge. But there were treasures hidden among the trash. Three lives, two of them more important to Mack Bolan than the third, but all inviolate while he survived, his honor pledged to bring them out intact...or die in the attempt.

Sally Palmer.

Nino Tattaglia.

Dave Eritrea.

He might have let Eritrea die, chalking it up as payment in arrears for ancient crimes, but after meeting Sarah, knowing of Brognola's promise that exclusive testimony would be bought with sanctuary, Bolan had no righteous choice.

The outer wall of Minelli's hard site posed no problem for the Executioner. He vaulted it and landed in a combat crouch inside, instinctively staying in the shadows there, his senses probing for any hostile challenge, finding none. When he was satisfied at last, the soldier cautiously advanced across the gently rolling, sparsely wooded grounds, his Uzi up and ready. Navigating by his instincts and the information gathered from his survey of the grounds that afternoon, he put a hundred yards behind him prior to meeting any opposition.

The *capo* had his sentries out, predictably, and they were circling the grounds in teams of two and three, one man in each team carrying a shotgun or an automatic weapon. Bolan heard the first pair coming and he melted into a shadow, letting them pass within arm's length; they suspected nothing. He had other games in mind just now.

The kind you carry home alive.

His mission was a dual one, incorporating life *and* death. Before he got around to dealing death, he had to find Eritrea and Sally Palmer, see them safely from the line of fire. And failing that...

The Executioner had long abandoned private hatred of the enemy as motivation for his war, but he had never shed the righteous wrath that came from finding a malignant cancer feeding on society, devouring the innocent and spitting out their mangled dreams as so much offal.

And the soldier hated, sure.

He carried cold, abiding hate inside him for all the pain and suffering that savages inflicted on their victims in a world of "civilized" and "cultured" men.

He hated all the waste—of lives, of dreams, of sheer humanity—which was the grim debris of war everlasting.

And worst of all, he hated the idea of dying while his enemies remained behind, to work their will, unhindered by a set of antiquated laws and handcuffed law-enforcement agencies.

He hated the idea of losing and yet recognized there could be no lasting victory.

He let the sentries pass, and others in their turn, until he stood in the shadow of the trees, no more than fifty yards away from Minelli's house, which was ablaze with lights. The cottages were to his right, the vacated pool between them and the mansion. It would be an easy stroll.

Unless they spotted him.

Unless he got killed covering those fifty yards.

And Bolan knew he had no choice. There was a single option open to him now, and only one direction he could travel in.

Forward.

BILL RAFFERTY COASTED THE LAST HUNDRED YARDS with his lights off, braking gently and killing the unmarked cruiser's engine when the Minelli gatehouse came into view. In his rearview mirror, he saw other blacked-out cars lining up, parking on the shoulder.

The young strike-force lieutenant shifted restlessly beside him, stubbing out his cigarette.

"Well, are we going in or what?"

"Or what. We wait until I give the word."

The young lieutenant lapsed into disgruntled silence, firing up another smoke. Bill Rafferty could sympathize, but how could he explain what was really going on?

No sweat, kid, we're just waiting for the Executioner to take some *capos* out, and then we'll bag whatever's left. We're batting cleanup, son.

Really.

So far, he was still on solid ground. The tip from Bolan had been logged and taped anonymously, and he was responding in due course. Without a warrant, he was technically required to sit and wait until reports of an incipient assassination on the grounds were proven true...or false. Once shots were fired, with other lawmen as his witnesses, he wouldn't need the warrant anyway.

And then it would get sticky.

For Rafferty, the task would be to hold his men in check and let the firefight run its course—just long enough for Bolan to achieve his goals. Five minutes, give or take, and it could be a lifetime, with thirty strike-force raiders chafing at the bit and ready for a little hellfire of their own.

There would be questions, certainly, unless he managed to finesse the play somehow and make the delay look natural. If someone started asking...

Rafferty shrugged off the threat, its consequences. He had made his choice, but he knew the NYPD dealt severely with its own when they malfunctioned in the field.

He marveled at the swift turn of events that placed him there, outside the Minelli gates, prepared to sacrifice career and reputation in the cause of Bolan's private war.

The war was getting personal again for Captain Rafferty, and with the sudden revelation came the thought that it had been impersonal for too damned long.

The Bolan concept was an ancient one...so damned old-fashioned it was downright revolutionary in its impact on a weak society, besieged by enemies within and terrorists without.

If someone terrorized your family, attempted to destroy your world, you'd kill the bastard and get on with the job of living. If other savages returned to take his place, and others after them, you'd organize a warrior class to scourge them from the earth and keep them living scared, out there among the jackals of the wasteland.

Minelli was small enough beginning, but his sheer existence was a rank affront to civilized society. If there was anything Bill Rafferty could do to wipe that stain away, he was prepared to spend his life in the attempt.

20

Bolan chose his moment, waiting until the patrolling sentries had passed from sight. He knew the risks, but the doomsday numbers were already running in his head and he was out of time.

He sprinted across the fifty yards of open ground and slid into the shadow of the nearest bungalow, the Uzi braced against his hip. Bolan circled toward the only cottage with a light still showing through its windows. He figured it had to be Dave Eritrea's prison cell.

The other bungalows were dark, their occupants inside the great house now. If someone had remained behind, outside, it would not be by choice, and Bolan navigated by the gut as he proceeded through the darkness toward his chosen target.

Past the bungalow that Sally Palmer shared with Patriarcca.

Past two others, silent, empty.

If Eritrea was inside the lighted cottage, then a portion of Bolan's job was done. He could release the informer, see him safely to the outer wall, then resume his long night's work with one load lifted from his mind. He might be under guard, of course, and Bolan let the Uzi hang against his chest as he approached his destination, opting for the silenced 93-R in case he had to deal with rear-guard watchmen prematurely.

It was far too early yet for Bolan to announce his presence. Any killing done on Dave Eritrea's behalf would have to be the silent kind, at least until Bolan had his major targets all together, in position for the slaughter.

Bolan finally emerged from midnight shadow, glancing each way before he moved into the light. The window shades were down, preventing his looking inside the bungalow, and something in the soldier's gut was gnawing at him, telling him that something was wrong somehow.

And still, he had no choice.

A flying kick above the flimsy lock propelled the thin door backward until it tore off its hinges. The warrior quickly entered, sleek Beretta leading, ready to accommodate all challengers.

The empty cottage mocked him with its silence.

Bolan swiftly closed the door behind him, checked the tiny bathroom and holstered the 93-R. It took a heartbeat for his eyes to find the handcuffs, empty now, still dangling from the cot positioned in a corner.

Eritrea was gone.

And Bolan knew he was too late.

Don Minelli was proceeding with his meeting on schedule, and he had the entertainment ready for his guests inside the mansion. It would require some time to check the other bungalows, but Bolan's instinct was telling him that he would find his other quarry—Flasher—in the manor house, as well.

The cannibals had gathered for their feast, and there would be no dearth of human appetizers on the menu. Unless another chef could unexpectedly interfere just long enough to make some alterations.

And the Executioner intended to supply a few hot dishes of his own.

He had already spent the day preparing appetites and setting party moods in Jersey, all around New York, and he did not intend to be excluded from final preparations for the bash. He might be short an invitation, but it was the thought that counted, after all...and Bolan's thoughts were bent on hellfire.

If Dave Eritrea and Sally Palmer were inside the mansion, he would have to get them clear before he brought the house down. Bill Rafferty might have an angle there...providing that he kept their date.

Bolan had the lawman pegged as a soldier of the same side. And the warrior needed help, the kind that Rafferty could provide. But any decision made by the captain was his own.

There could be no draftees in Bolan's holy war. The price of entry was commitment, sure.

Bill Rafferty would know that going in, and he would enter with his eyes wide open, or he would not come in at all.

It was the only way to fight a holy war.

The only way for holy warriors to survive.

Tonight, perhaps, it might be the only way to die.

Turning the lights off, Mack Bolan left the bungalow and moved toward the house.

"So, Ducks, let's have the story, eh? What's eatin' Jules?"

The crew chief, Tommy Fiorini, shifted on the Lincoln's front seat to find a comfortable position for his ample backside. Never fond of traveling, he was uncomfortable here, in hostile territory, riding in a strange car through unfriendly darkness.

"Nothin' special," Fiorini told his wheelman, hoping that he might convince himself, as well. "They had some kinda beef when he showed up, an' anyway, he wants a little show of force, tha's all."

But was it all?

Fiorini hadn't liked the tone of Patriarcca's voice when they had spoken on the telephone, and there had been the sense of something left unsaid, as if his *capo* feared there might be others listening on the line.

So what the hell else was new?

Somebody had been listening to the brotherhood now for as long as Fiorini could remember. Feds, the local cops, some blasted prosecutor or a senator's committee. Any time you needed headlines, or some new appropriations for the yearly budget, all you had to do was holler Mafia and leak some tapes to get exactly what you wanted from the purse-string boys.

In Fiorini's younger days, it had been different, though. There had been definite security in signing on with one of the established families, making your bones and taking the oath by candlelight, with your friends and family looking on.

It had begun to change back in the sixties when Kennedy was in the White House. Things had gone from bad to worse since then, despite some real good times along the way. Fiorini had picked up the nickname Ducks back in 1963, when he was busted and convicted on a contrived federal charge of exceeding his limit on killing migratory water fowl.

A frigging duck conviction, for cryin' out loud, and it had followed him these twenty years, until it didn't make him see red anymore when someone called him Ducks. He laughed it off now, and hardly gave a thought to ripping out the driver's lungs.

But there was no surefire security, not any more. The Feds were everywhere, and even granting that the brotherhood's worst enemy, that bastard Bolan, had gone up in smoke a few years back, the syndicate had never quite recovered from the damage it sustained when he was still alive and kicking ass.

Minelli's meeting was designed to fix all that and put the territories back together, better than they were before. And Fiorini knew that Jules was skeptical—of Don Minelli's leadership, at any rate—but still, you had to give the guy his due for putting all of it together.

Patriarcca was an old-style *capo*, and he shied away from new ideas unless they made him plenty money with a minimum of risk. He had begun to see Minelli's rise as some kind of a threat to his own West Coast empire, and while Fiorini didn't really grasp the logic of it all, he had been smart enough to keep from thinking for himself, to keep on playing smart and taking orders.

From his entry to the brotherhood, Fiorini realized that he had not been marked by destiny to ride the throne. His role as Patriarcca's regional commander fit him fine, and he was glad to do the old man's bidding, but damn, he hated traveling.

The crew chief swiveled ponderously in his seat and craned to look across his shoulder, past the gunners in the back seat, through the broad rear window of the Continental. Running close behind them, four more tanks were bearing gunners to the meeting, bringing in the cavalry to make Don Patriarcca feel secure.

It would make Don Minelli as mad as hell, but the crew chief thought his boys could hold their own if it came down to any kind of heavy action. He had picked them with the same discerning eye he had for women, passing over those who showed a trace of weakness or reluctance when it came to dirty work.

But Ducks was hoping that it would not come to killing there, on foreign soil, where his connections stood for nothing and he had no place to run in case it all went wrong. Back home, around Seattle, he could count on grease with cops and politicians, on his *capo*'s help, but here...

The crew chief shook his momentary doubts away and sat up straighter in his seat. The old man would have told him if a war was in the wings. This little bit of flexing would establish Patriarcca as a man of substance, nothing more, and if Minelli didn't like it, well, the upstart don could just go screw himself. He was a kid, when you came down to it, still wet behind the ears, no matter if his family was twice as

large as Patriarcca's, man for man. He didn't have the
strong connections Jules had, up and down the coast back
home.

"So, how much farther is it?"

"Couple of miles," the wheelman told him. "Ought to
see it soon."

The crew chief checked his watch and sighed.

Another couple of miles. Six long hours on his butt had
made him stiff.

Tommy Fiorini settled back, puffing busily on his cigar,
and concentrated on the darkened road ahead. A few more
minutes, and he could relax...or really start to sweat.

ERNESTO MINELLI TAPPED A FORK against his wineglass,
waited for the murmuring of voices to die down. When it
was silent, he stood up, surveying faces ranged along each
side of the extended conference table.

On his left and right, close by, the other New York dons
were watching with a mixture of distrust and curiosity. He
gave up looking for a message in the faces, realizing all of
them had suffered losses through the day, aware that some
suspected him of being at the bottom of it all.

D'Antoni, from New Jersey, glowered through a screen
of thick cigar smoke, big hands clenched together on the
table, fingers working nervously. The hands were band-
aged, making Minelli wonder just exactly what form Bobby's "accident" that afternoon had taken...but he pushed
it out of mind, glancing around the table, reading faces,
moods.

No thaw from Patriarcca or his shadow, Cigliano—but
the New York *capo* had expected none. They would resist
him, almost certainly, no matter how he broached the subject on his mind, and he would have to deal with their hostility later. Soon, now, he thought. Quite soon.

The others watched him noncommittally, adopting out-
ward attitudes of wait and see. Chicago's Paulo Vaccarelli

sat near Santos Bataglia, out of Boston, both men smoking and staring at him, faces impassive. Across the table, Miami's Jerry Lazia was stationed next to Vince Galante, speaking for the Kansas City-Cleveland axis. Finally, and closest, Aguirre of the New York end, were representatives of old Don Narozine's Baltimore contingent, waiting for the show to start.

The audience was in, and it was up to Don Ernesto to win them over...or, at least, to stall the hostiles long enough to give himself some breathing room.

His smile included all of them—friend and enemy, the vast majority who were still uncommitted. When he spoke, his voice was firm and strong.

"I'm happy all of you could make it here tonight, despite the recent troubles." A general grumbling around the table let him know that he had touched on the subject of their chief concern. "We had some trouble here, ourselves, as Jules and Lester there could tell you, eh?"

No gesture of acknowledgment from either of the West Coast dons. He forged ahead, ignoring the snub.

"The reason I asked you all to join me here was so that we could settle some unfinished business. What I've got to say pertains to everybody in this room...and I believe you're gonna think the trip was worth it when you've heard me out."

A pause then, for effect, to let the appetizer settle in and whet their curiosity. No need to drop it on them all at once. There would be time enough for raking in the honors when he had them on his side.

"We've had a lotta trouble lately—hell, the past few years—with yellow rats who've sold out to the government and carried tales about our families, this thing of ours."

A murmur, this time of agreement, ran around the table.

"Fact is," he told them when the rumbling had died away, "nobody's had more trouble with informers than we have right here...and you know who I mean."

A growl this time, and not just from the New York dons. The shock waves from the testimony of the rat he had in mind had reached from coast to coast, and Minelli knew he had their full attention now.

"This bastard grew up not five miles from here, wormed his way up through the family, and then he *turned*, like some...some kinda fucking snake or something, biting at the hand that fed him all those years. I know; he bit my family more than once, and I got scars to show for it."

No need to mention that Dave Eritrea's testimony also cleared the throne that Minelli hoped to occupy this night.

"There's been a lot of talk about what should be done with rats like these...and this rat in particular...but no one's got a handle on exactly where the Feds were hiding them away. So far."

An air of expectation filled the conference room, and Minelli took his time, maintaining eye contact with the two Aces standing watch on a side door, waiting for his command. At a nod, one of them disappeared through the exit, hastening to fetch his prize.

"Well...I got lucky, or, maybe I just touched some bases nobody had touched before. Whatever, it's my pleasure now to introduce a special guest who couldn't join us earlier. You could say he was all tied up for dinner."

At a snap of his fingers, the side door was opened, and the Black Ace propelled Eritrea into the room. The hostage staggered, found his balance and was blinking at the faces ranged around the table when a howl went up and everyone was jabbering together in excited tones.

On Minelli's left, Vito Aguirre was out of his seat in an instant, landing two quick punches on Eritrea's jaw before his *consigliere* and one of the Aces could restrain him, leading him gently back to his chair. The other *capos* kept their seats, but they were glowering darkly at the new arrival—and most of them were viewing Minelli with a new respect.

The mafioso raised a hand to still the uproar, waiting while it ran its course.

"You'll get your chance," he promised them. "Fact is, I figured some of you could use a little after-dinner entertainment, eh? Work off a little of that pasta while you got the chance."

He shared their laughter, glancing at Eritrea from the corner of one eye and nodding for the Ace to lead him out.

"He'll be around, don't worry...but there's other business that we need to talk about before we break it up." He hesitated, took a breath and plunged ahead. "Like how this thing of ours has fallen all apart the past few years, for instance. And like what it's gonna take to make it like it was before."

They were listening now, but some of them were still openly skeptical, as if they knew what was coming and were determined not to buy it. Minelli refused to let that deter him. He had come too far out on the limb to back down now.

"It used to be the brotherhood was run like a machine, well oiled, well kept, no problems that you couldn't fix without a major overhaul. Time was, the dons sat down together just like one, and what they said...well, shit, that was the fucking *law*. Some judge, some congressman, whatever, tries to screw around with the brothers, and he finds himself out of a job. He keeps coming, and he gets his frigging head handed to him on a platter, am I right?"

A murmur of assent, and even Cigliano nodded, getting in the spirit of it now and thinking back to good old days that he had never known himself.

"Time was, we ran this country...and we could again...but not the way we operate right now." He paused and let them glance around at one another, silently condemning this or that of their associates for weakening the standards of the whole. "Today, it's like a Chinese fire drill when we try to get things done. The Feds are up our ass, holes with a magnifying glass, and all we do is shake our heads like some lame ducks who haven't got the legs to stand and fight.''

Dead silence, and no one among them dared to clear his throat, thereby attracting notice to himself. The time had come to spell it out. He swallowed hard and went ahead.

"I say we need a leader, like we used to have. Somebody who could guide the brotherhood. We useta have a man like that. You all know who I mean."

"Damn right." The rumble came from Bonadonna, on his right. "That Augie Marinello was a *man*."

The *capo* nodded, using all the strength of will to keep the smile off his burning face.

"We need a man like that today. We need what he can give us, right up front, the way it used to be."

Down at the far end of the table, Patriarcca cleared his throat loudly.

"You got some way to raise the dead that we ain't heard of, Ernie?"

L.Λ. Lester snickered, joined by several of the others. Minelli kept his face impassive, fighting the urge to snap back at the Washington *capo*.

"That won't be necessary, Jules. The Marinello line is still alive."

For a moment the silence was deafening, then it broke, and everyone was babbling. Halfway down the table, old Tom Gregorio was pounding on the woodwork with his fist, shouting the others down, demanding the floor, and it was several moments before the noise died and he could be heard. When he got his chance he lurched erect, leaning toward his host with both fists on the tabletop.

"You're movin' kinda fast for some of us, Ernesto. Last I heard, Augie didn't leave no sons."

"His wife was childless, Tom. That doesn't mean he died without an heir."

"So where's this heir?" Gregorio demanded. "Let him show himself."

"You're looking at him, Thomas."

"Bullshit!" Patriarcca shouted from his seat, and then the other voices drowned him out, all clamoring at once with questions, exclamations, statements of surprise or disbelief. The *capo* raised both hands, waiting a full five minutes before he had the chance to speak below a shout.

"I realize how difficult this is for some of you to handle, but I have the evidence you need, and all of you will be permitted, naturally, to check it out before you leave. I've got letters, written to my mother in the don's own hand, along with other papers and a diary left by Barney Matilda. Some of you know how close he was to Augie; they came up together through the ranks."

Gregorio was still on his feet, but his hands were no longer clenched into fists. They hung by his sides, and he had a stunned expression on his face.

"Supposing what you say is true...supposing, now...how come you been hidin' your light under a bushel all these years?"

"My father kept on hoping for an heir that he could claim until...the day he died. After that, well, with our friend Eritrea in the saddle, and some others I could name, I wanted some security before I stuck my neck out. That make sense to you, Tom?"

"Yeah." The older don still sounded bewildered. "It makes sense, but..."

Minelli smiled.

"Again, I understand your reservations...and I hope the evidence I have will answer them. If not..."

Patriarcca leaned across the table, jabbing a finger toward Minelli. He was pale, but his resistance was unshaken.

"Let's cut through all the hearts and flowers here," he snarled. "Suppose you are exactly who you say. So what?

What makes you think you're fit to guide this thing of ours?''

Minelli stiffened.

"I've got the blood," he answered. "When I bagged Eritrea, I proved I had the brains. If it comes down to that, I've got the troops."

"Aha!"

Patriarcca lurched to his feet, but before he could make his point, the muffled sound of an explosion reached their ears from somewhere outside. A minor shock wave rattled the curtained windows in their frames. An instant later, automatic weapons joined the chorus, firing from the direction of the bungalows.

"What kind of shit is this?"

"Hey, what the hell—"

Minelli left his place, moving down the length of the table, motioning for the Aces to follow. As he passed among the other dons, he raised his voice, trying to sound reassuring.

"Nothing to worry about," he told them, wishing he believed it as he spoke the words. "If it's the bastard who hit us today, we'll have two heads instead of one."

The second blast was closer—close enough, in fact, to smash the giant picture window, spraying fractured slivers through the drapes and peppering the walls, the guests, with flying glass.

And Don Ernesto Minelli saw his world begin to teeter on its axis, tilting, slipping through his fingers just as he began to think it was secure. He reached the door, the Aces on his heels, and he was running in the direction of the gunfire, his pulse hammering inside his skull.

He would not lose it now, when he was this close.

He *could* not.

He would die first, if that was what it took.

But no way would he die alone.

21

Mack Bolan had kept his distance from the lighted swimming-pool area, circling warily around the flagstone patio, homing in on the French doors that would give him access to the manor and the men inside. He had set the Uzi on automatic mode, prepared to lay down cover fire in case he should be spotted prematurely by a roving sentry.

And the Executioner had covered half the distance to the house before it happened.

Deviating from his rounds, a gunner suddenly appeared on Bolan's flank, emerging from the shadows into the misty pool light, one hand tugging at his fly, the other making sure his shirttail was tucked in. The guy had obviously had a call of nature, but his face was registering grim surprise and another kind of message as he spotted Bolan focusing upon the little stutter gun he held.

The guy was good, you had to give him that. Within a heartbeat's time he let the zipper go and scrambled for his holstered side arm, finding it and almost clearing leather in the time allowed.

But almost was not quite good enough to keep the guy alive.

Mack Bolan crouched and swung out his stubby chopper, tightening into the squeeze as he made target acquisition. The Uzi stuttered and half a dozen parabellum manglers hissed across the surface of the pool in search of flesh and bone.

The gunner did a jerky little dance before he folded, wallowing beside the pool in his own blood slick. His dying spasms brought him to the brink, and as Mack Bolan watched, the carcass toppled over, disappearing into the deep end.

The gunfire had attracted other sentries, and he heard them in the darkness, converging on him, startled voices calling back and forth behind the bungalows, among the trees, beyond the house. The nearest were at Bolan's back, and he was swiveling to meet them when the first dark form materialized, stepping from shadow near the bungalow once occupied by Sally Palmer and her mark.

Carrying a shotgun, the guard didn't bother aiming it once he had the black-clad warrior in view. The pump gun roared, and Bolan dodged a gust of buckshot, toppling a metal picnic table, wincing as an errant pellet burned across his thigh. The sound of the table hitting the ground rang in his ears, and a second blast in rapid-fire destroyed the brightly striped umbrella.

The warrior wriggled on his stomach, Uzi probing out ahead of him, intent on getting clear before the gunner and his cronies had a better chance to find their range. Perforated by the shotgun blasts, the table was a flimsy shield at best, and it would not stand up to any concentrated small-arms fire.

He found an opening and pegged a short burst at the sniper, missing him by a few feet, but it was still enough to drive him back and give Bolan time to move. As he jumped up and broke from cover, he tossed a frag grenade, winding up the pitch and letting fly by instinct, all the while on the run.

He did not have to mark the progress of his high-explosive egg to know that it was flying true. Experience and practice had prepared him for the move. The soldier was a dozen yards away and sliding behind another table—this one built of redwood—when the night was torn apart by smoky thunder.

Bolan's ears, ringing from the blast, picked up strangled screams and the twanging sound of shrapnel overhead. His eyes searched the darkness for other human targets. Three of them were closing on his left, another two were about to outflank him on the right. He would be surrounded unless he broke the circle and finally made it to the manor house.

A blazing figure eight of Uzi fire caught two of his assailants on the left, and drove their comrade under cover on the far side of the swimming pool. With a half turn to the right, Bolan brought the others under fire, rewarded by a muffled gasp as one of them had both legs cut from under him and collapsed across the line of fire, dead before he could scream.

His partner, doing a flying shoulder roll, lost his carbine, coming up behind a chaise longue empty-handed and digging for the pistol on his hip. The Executioner squeezed off another burst, his parabellum manglers chewing through the plastic and aluminum construction of the deck chair, boring through the gunner's chest, blowing him backward. As blood sputtered from his chest, his boot heels drummed on the deck for a second, then stopped.

The survivors had worked out Bolan's range by now, and another pair of guns had joined them, sniping from the darkness, bullets chipping at his redwood barricade. Another moment, and the hostiles would have enough gunners to rush him, sacrificing their lives to overwhelm him with their numbers and finish Bolan off.

He had to move, and there was only one way left to go.

The house.

The Uzi spit out a ragged burst that raked the patio with flying death, and Bolan fed a brand-new magazine into the pistol grip. A fresh grenade in his hand, he brought his legs up, gathering his strength for what would be the final run to cover—or instant death.

The soldier was about to move when shadowy figures stirred behind the French doors and someone pulled back the drapes, opened the latch and swung the portal back. He raked the windows with a burst, waist high, and threw the grenade inside.

He ran into the blast, bullets snapping at his heels, and launched into a headlong dive that carried him through the shattered doors to the littered carpet within. Concussion rocked him, squeezed the wind from his lungs. Broken glass was everywhere, its sharp fangs ripping at his hands, his face, his clothing. Unmindful of the pain, he wriggled through the rain of shrapnel and plaster clinging grimly to the stutter gun. He glanced around, seeking temporary haven from the gunners who were closing in behind him like a pack of hungry dogs.

He had perhaps only a moment left to meet them and turn their charge around before it overwhelmed him, carried him away.

A moment to determine if he would live or die.

Either way, the dying there was far from over.

In fact, it was only beginning.

THE WHEELMAN BROUGHT THE CAR TO A HALT outside the gates as Tommy Fiorini concentrated on the gateman. There were others hanging back behind him in the darkness, watching, and the crew chief could have sworn he caught the glint of moonlight on their weapons as they jockeyed for position.

Frowning, he wondered what the hell was going on with so much iron around the gates. Security would be important, sure, with all the dons inside, but after Jules had made his call...

A graveyard breeze blew down the open neck of Tommy's shirt.

Suppose the call had been about these guns on the gate? Suppose Minelli had taken it wrong...or Jules had been trying to alert his troops, but couldn't come right out and say that he was under house arrest? Suppose the families were already at war, and Jules was dead? What then?

The crew chief reined in his grim imagination. His palms were moist and clammy. He did not want to die out there, so far from home.

"Heads up," he told the boys in back.

The gateman was approaching, and Fiorini beckoned him to the passenger's side and cranked down the window. He put on a friendly grin, but in the darkness of the car, his fist was wrapped around the Army-issue .45 he wore beneath his armpit, ready if the stranger made an unexpected move.

"Excuse me, sir. Were you expected?"

"Well, I couldn't really say," Ducks replied, grinning. "My boss, he's in there with the others, for the sit-down, 'kay? I get this call, an' he says hop the next flight out. Some kinda party goin' on, I guess."

The gateman shot a glance across his shoulder toward the watchers in the shadows.

"We weren't expecting anybody else tonight," he said. "Who was it made that call again?"

Tommy Fiorini let his smile slip a notch, the barest touch of ice edging into his voice.

"Don Patriarcca, from Seattle. Hey, we been a long time in the air, a long time drivin' out. There can't be any beef if we just find a place to park, some coffee, hey?"

"I'll have to call the house and get it cleared."

"You do that."

Tommy Ducks was staring at the gateman's back, beginning to crank the window up, when an explosion sounded. Muffled by distance, it sounded to the crew chief like a small grenade or the world's biggest cherry bomb.

"Hey, what the fuck—"

The wheelman reached inside his coat for the .38 in his belt, and Tommy had his Army-issue ready as the gateman stiffened, freezing in his tracks. The automatic-weapons fire was unmistakably from the mansion, and something sure as hell was coming down around their ears.

And Jules was in there!

Holy shit!

His piece out the window, Tommy Ducks sighted on the gateman's shoulder blades and fired, the autoloader bucking in his fist. The straw man flopped on his face. The others dodged farther behind the tall gates, out of sight.

"Let's hit it!"

The driver pressed the pedal to the floor, and the Continental slammed against the gates, breaking through, the other crew wagons close behind. Tommy Ducks had a fleeting impression of *other* cars behind those sleek shadows, sharklike, closing fast—and one of them was turning on its red light, announcing its occupants for what they were.

The cops, for cryin' out loud!

"Keep going, dammit!"

Tommy Ducks still had a job to do, and if the frigging cops got in his way, he'd have to step on them. Just like at home, and never mind that he was now three thousand miles away from safety, from the cops he knew.

They didn't make 'em bulletproof in old New York, and Tommy Ducks could still match slugs with any man alive, given half a chance.

Which was, the crew chief thought, almost exactly what they had.

CROUCHING IN FRONT OF THE WOMAN with pliers in his hand, Lazarus froze at the first sound of gunfire outside. He hesitated, glancing back and forth from her battered face and shredded, gaping blouse to the man stationed at the door to guarantee his privacy.

The Black Ace frowned, wondering exactly what the hell was going on. Throughout the day, he had been less than totally impressed with Minelli's security precautions and his responses to the danger they faced, and now he would not be surprised if the sentries on the grounds had opened fire on one another.

Downstairs, the would-be boss of bosses was engaged in blowing his own horn, while out on the yard...

The first explosion reached him almost as an echo, and he moved to the window as a second blast shook the house.

Forget about the yardmen, then. Not even Minelli would be fool or paranoid enough to issue them grenades.

They were under attack, and that made it Lazarus's job to defend the manor house and its occupants from any outside threat.

The Ace smiled scornfully as he tossed the pliers toward a nearby table. He reached inside his jacket, withdrew a Browning Hi-Power automatic pistol and worked the slide, chambering a live round, lowering the hammer with his thumb before he stowed the piece.

The gunfire was inside now, raging in the downstairs corridors, and Lazarus knew he might already be too late. If the enemy had come in force, if one or more of the local families had risen against Minelli...

The *capo*'s words came back to him with ringing clarity. "If this thing falls apart, we all go down, your precious Aces, everything."

And Lazarus would need some life insurance, just in case.

The woman would do well for starters.

Steel flashed in his palm, and he cut through the bonds that held her arms behind the chair, ignoring her tattered blouse as he reached down to haul her erect, keeping her on her feet when she swayed, close to falling.

It took a moment for her to recover balance, find the strength to match his pace with clumsy feet. He half carried her toward the door, growling at his backup when the man moved too slowly to suit him. There was no time for sluggishness now, with all their lives at stake.

He smelled the smoke after they had left the small interrogation room, and Lazarus at once abandoned any thought of marshalling the last defense of Minelli's palace home. The *capo* could fend for himself, and Lazarus was bailing out while the getting was good.

It was survival of the fittest, but he could not afford to travel with the excess baggage he was holding now. If he was going to travel fast, then he would have to travel light.

He hesitated as they reached the top of the curving staircase, turning to his flanker, consternation written on his face.

"You take the point," he said.

The other gunner brushed past him, toward the stairs, and Lazarus let him lead, watched him descend the first few steps. Lazarus drew the Browning, thumbed back the hammer and sighted quickly down the slide.

One shot was all it took, the parabellum slug hitting left of center, blowing a rat hole in the gunner's skull and peeling back a strip of scalp before the body fell face-first down the stairs.

And he was starting downstairs when the woman made her sudden, unexpected move, both hands clasped tight around the dead gunner's dropped pistol, immobilizing the hammer and slide, as her knee whipped around to find Lazarus's groin with agonizing accuracy.

Lazarus was on his knees, his eyes screwed up against the pain, and she was kicking him, bare heel striking the bridge of his nose, drawing blood, driving him back on his haunches. Grunting, he struck out, and his left hand sank into yielding belly-flesh, expelling the wind from her lungs.

She staggered back, and his weapon was clear. He squeezed the trigger blindly, thunder in his ears, and heard the startled little scream as she toppled backward, thumping downstairs in the wake of a corpse, losing her weapon.

The goddamned bitch!

Lazarus struggled to his feet, clutching at his wounded genitals with one hand, dragging the Browning up with his other. He slumped against the banister, ignoring the hot blood that dribbled from his lips, blanking his mind against the painful throbbing in his groin.

Below, the woman was crouched beside the body of his former henchman, wrestling with the corpse and running one hand beneath the suit coat, frisking him for his side arm. If she reached it...

"Too late, bitch," he snarled.

He used both hands to raise the automatic and aim at the target.

His finger tightened on the Browning's trigger, and he smiled.

"HIT THE SIREN!"

Hunched across the steering wheel, his knuckles white, Rafferty stared at the taillights of the Lincoln ahead of him, his own accelerator on the floor. Beside him, the lieutenant keyed a switch beneath the dash, and a hysteric banshee wail began to emanate from somewhere out front, beneath the cruiser's hood.

Behind them, other sirens joined the chorus, Rafferty's commandos keeping up, two men jumping from the tail car to seize the gate guards, line them against the wall and keep them prisoner while the cavalry went in to do its stuff.

The driver of the rental limousine did not respond to the siren's call or Rafferty's cyclopean scarlet beacon mounted on the roof. Determined to keep pace with those ahead of him, the wheelman kept on pushing it, now running flat-out for the Minelli manor house along the curving graveled drive.

Rafferty heard the gunfire and explosions, despite the siren and his engine's whine. He knew that hell was coming down, and even though his entrance was somewhat premature, there was no way on earth to stall it once the guns went off back there around the gate.

It might be one thing to park outside the walls and listen for a moment to the distant sounds of combat from within, restraining his enthusiasm long enough to let Mack Bolan have a decent start, but it was something else when bodies started falling right before his eyes, with twenty other cops behind him, looking on.

Bill Rafferty had had no choice at all, and he was in it now for good or ill. He hoped the Executioner would hear him coming, know that it had fallen through and have time to clear out before the roof fell in.

The brake lights on the lead car, which was perhaps a hundred yards ahead, were winking as it pulled even with the house. Directly in his high beams, Rafferty saw a head pop out a window on the driver's side, pop back—and then the gunner had his shoulders through the opening, a shotgun in his hands.

And he was aiming at the goddamned cruiser.

Rafferty stood on the brake, instinctively twisting his wheel hard left, taking the charge on his side to spare the lieutenant. He heard the shotgun boom, the impact of its pellets on the door behind him, boring through and shredding fabric on the back seat, missing flesh by inches.

His passenger craned out and angled a shot across the windshield, the muzzle-flashes from his snubby side arm flaring with each shot. Rafferty ripped his own piece clear of leather, driving one-handedly, tailgating the Lincoln and battering it with his grill, throwing the shotgunner off balance. He had a fleeting glimpse of the gunner's weapon as he lost it while he went cartwheeling through the darkness.

The Continental swung wide, turning around in front of the house, sliding into line beside the other Lincolns. And doors were springing open all along the line, disgorging shapes into the night, armed figures sprinting for cover, some going toward the house, others turning back to face the screaming cruisers as they formed a secondary ring around the first.

A heavy slug ripped through the cruiser's grill and Rafferty could feel the engine die. He opened the door and rolled clear, leaving the high beams on to pin his targets at center stage. Crouched behind the door, he sought a target for his Magnum, sweeping the four-inch barrel back and forth until he found his mark.

A beefy soldier was squatting by the nearest limo, shooting at the house and then back toward the cruisers, with an Army-issue .45.

Rafferty watched the guy duck a shotgun blast, then fumbled briefly with the fresh magazine. The captain sighted down the Magnum's barrel, squeezing off in double action.

His target sat down hard, one fat hand coming up to cover what was left of the face, feeling briefly for the missing nose before the life went out of him and he collapsed backward on the bloody gravel.

Rafferty's blood was pounding in his ears as he sought another target, and another. Around him other weapons had joined the skirmish, automatic rifles and riot guns. The cavalry was weighing in, and they would not be stopped until they brought the curtain down this night.

And it was their war now, although they didn't know it yet, not really. They were fighting for their lives, and it would take some time, some education, for the strike-force men to know that they were also warring for a higher cause.

Bill Rafferty would find a way to tell them all about it, if he lived.

When the smoke cleared, Rafferty was well aware that he might find his own men there, among the dead and dying on the field. If so, well, there was nothing he could do about it but try to even up the score another day.

And he was counting on another day. This couldn't be the end of it, not now.

It couldn't be.

If there was any justice out there, this had to be a new beginning for them all.

22

Mack Bolan fed the stutter gun another magazine and wriggled back between the sofa and a capsized coffee table, doubling his legs beneath him, rising to a crouch. Beyond the makeshift barricade, a ring of hostile guns surrounded him, their hot converging fire almost sufficient now to root him out from cover and destroy him on the run.

Almost.

The Executioner was not done yet, and every passing heartbeat served as a reminder that his prey—the *capos* there convened—were slipping farther from his grasp.

Bolan knew that it was now or never. If he allowed the gunners to immobilize him there before he reached the kill-ground, he would have wasted his life.

And Bolan never wasted anything if there were viable alternatives.

He set the Uzi in front of him and from his pistol belt plucked a frag grenade with each hand. The greenish metal eggs were cool, their slick exteriors belying all the jagged death inside. Enough of fire and steel and smoky thunder there, he thought, to clear his road—assuming he could pull it off.

Bolan freed the pins and let them fall, firmly holding in the safety spoons. It would require precision timing, with a certain reckless disregard for all the odds arrayed against him. If Bolan faltered, hesitated in the least, then he would die. It was that simple.

The soldier picked out his targets by their sound, memorizing their locations for future reference. There would be no damn time at all to spot them when he made his move, and Bolan knew that if he missed his targets by a yard or more, assorted furniture would bear the brunt of the explosions and neutralize the fire and thunder that seemed to be his only hope.

He moved, and hostile weapons were already barking at him as he showed himself. A .38 drew blood beneath one upraised arm, and semiautomatic rifle slugs were chewing up the coffee table, searching for him.

Bolan pitched left, then right, and the eggs were airborne, spiraling along separate flight paths. He ducked under cover, grunting as a rifle bullet plowed a bloody track across his shoulder blade.

He kept his balance, scooping up the Uzi, holding it against his chest so he would be ready for the hellfire moment that was coming.

Now! And the explosives detonated almost simultaneously, sharp concussions battering his barricade and rocking Bolan on his haunches, filling the air above his head with singing shards of steel. No time to wait; he was on his feet, already moving as the hostile gunners tried to understand precisely what was happening to them.

Three of them no longer cared. Their mutilated bodies lay where they had fallen, twisted by the shock waves, punctured by the storm of shrapnel. Bolan put them out of mind now, concentrating on survivors. Four were visible, the nearest staggering around in circles, fresh blood streaming down his face from ragged scalp wounds. He was struggling to raise the nickel-plated pistol in his hands.

He never made it. Bolan's submachine gun chattered briefly, and a sizzling wreath of parabellum manglers settled on the target's shoulders, drilling flesh and bone and fabric, turning bloodied face into a screaming death mask.

Bolan was already moving as the headless body toppled back into an easy chair.

The Uzi tracked on, spitting lethal indignation at its human targets, mowing down a gunner who fought to rise, his shotgun awkward in hands almost devoid of fingers. Kneeling, a third was tracking the warrior with an automatic pistol when the hell storm broke around him, punched him over backward, out of sight and out of mind.

On the run, the remaining gunner winged a shot at Bolan, his bullet shattering a vase somewhere behind the Executioner. Two loping strides, and the gunner was almost to the kitchen door, almost to sanctuary, when he stumbled on a string of parabellums, slammed face-first against the wall and smeared it with his dying essence.

Bolan scanned the battlefield, moving out of there in search of other prey—the *capos*, right—when he heard a scream on the stairs.

A female voice, as hurt and angry as it was afraid.

He reached the staircase at a run, found Sally Palmer crouched upon the first-floor landing, wrestling a pistol from its holster underneath a dead man's arm. He was about to call her name when movement on the stairs alerted him to danger, and he spied a gunner with his Browning braced in both hands, sighting on the lady Fed.

Bolan swept the Uzi up, squeezing off as the target entered his sights. Three rounds ripped out in rapid fire and then the bolt locked open, smoking, frozen on the empty chamber.

On the stairs Bolan's target staggered, jerking with the impact as a single bullet burrowed through his rib cage, throwing off his aim. The banister absorbed the other rounds. There was fight enough inside him yet to do some lethal damage here before he died. The Browning wavered, torn between two targets, finally choosing Bolan, centering upon his upturned face.

The soldier didn't waste time with his stutter gun. He thumbed off the safety as his arm extended rising to the classic dueling stance, his body angled to narrow the hostile gunner's target zone. But before he could fire, Sally Palmer brought her captured weapon into play and squeezed off in rapid fire, the echo of her pistol filling the stairwell.

Her target twisted, fell back against the banister, his gun arm drooping out of line. He was either dead or nearly dead, right, but there was no damned point in taking any chances. Bolan's bullet drilled into his forehead between the staring eyes. The gunner's head snapped back, and he plunged over the railing backward, the lady Fed continuing to fire until the slide locked open on her weapon and it wouldn't answer any more.

Mack Bolan joined her on the landing, gently pried the smoking weapon from her grasp and helped her to her feet.

"It's over, Sal," he told her, and her eyes focused for the first time on his face, the tears already etching tracks across her cheeks.

And she had been through hell, no doubt about it. Bolan knew the signs—and knew, as well, that she had come through relatively clean, all things considered. Any longer, though...

A banging door beneath them severed Bolan's morbid train of thought. One long stride brought him to the banister. Below, a clutch of frightened men rushed from the conference room. Their plan seemed to be to cross Bolan's private battlefield and reach the hoped-for security of the cars parked out front.

He recognized some of the men—most of them, at any rate—and put names to them as they trooped below him. Bonadonna and Gregorio. Reina and Aguirre. Vaccarelli and D'Antoni. Patriarcca and Galante. Lazia and Cigliano.

And Tattaglia, sure.

The little mafioso-turned-informant was the first to spot Mack Bolan poised above them, the Beretta held in front of him as if to bless the throng. His reaction made the others notice. Pallid faces swiveled around to recognize their doom, the shock of recognition registered differently on each countenance.

A dozen faces, give or take, and fourteen rounds still nestled in Bolan's silenced Beretta.

He leaned across the railing and exchanged a knowing glance with Tattaglia. The little mafioso nodded almost imperceptibly and closed his eyes.

The parabellum bullet drilled his shoulder, high and clean, its exit clear of bone and vital organs, any major arteries. The impact spun him like a top and dumped him facedown on the carpet, outside the line of fire as the Executioner got down to lethal business with his prey.

The *capos* scattered, fanning out in all directions, but the warrior took his time and did it right. There was no room for error.

Gregorio was sprinting back into the conference room when swift death overtook him, drilling between his shoulder blades and spouting blood before he toppled on his face, momentum carrying his dead weight on between the open doors.

Aguirre and Reina were running hell-bent for the safety of the kitchen, too damned far away to do them any good, and straining all the same. A silent double punch reached out to tap their shoulders, ramming them together and throwing both men off balance, their arms and legs entangled as they sprawled in a lethal embrace.

Frank Bonadonna began to draw a pistol from his belt, then remembered he didn't have one as a parabellum mangler punched his face inward, transforming it into a collapsing rubber mask that bore no trace of its original humanity.

D'Antoni *had* a gun, but there was no time for him to use it as a silent round drilled through his throat, disintegrating larynx and esophagus, its passage opening the floodgates of his jugular to leave the mobster gagging, drowning in his own blood.

The Windy City *capo*, Paulie Vaccarelli, also had a weapon, and he cleared his holster with it, squeezing off a single round skyward, dying on his feet as Bolan drilled him through the forehead, blowing brains and all the rotten rest of him away.

Miami's Jerry Lazia and Cleveland's Vince Galante made their break together, racing for the broad French doors and patio beyond, but Bolan never let them get there, squeezing off two rounds that pitched them both headlong into the awkward, tumbling sprawl of death.

L.A. Lester Cigliano tried to stick with Patriarcca, but the older don brushed past him in his panic, elbowing the younger man and knocking him off balance. He was down on one knee when the parabellum drilled his temple, wiping out his anger, fear and life in one searing pain.

The *capo* of Seattle was a plodding form, almost grotesque, his back presented to the marksman as a perfect target. Mack Bolan thought of Sally as he flicked the fireselector switch to automatic mode and raised the 93-R, braced in both hands, the sights immediately lining up between thick shoulder blades and rising to include the ruddy, balding skull. A squeeze...and three rounds rippled out of there, virtually decapitating Patriarcca on impact, depositing his faceless body belly-down across a bloodied, shrapnel-punctured couch.

And it was over, right, except for Don Minelli, who had put it all together in the first place. Feeding the Beretta with another magazine, he turned to Sally Palmer. She stood, head down, leaning against the wall. Her arms were wrapped around her, as if to give her warmth. If she had observed the massacre, she gave no sign.

"I need Minelli and Eritrea," he told her simply, waiting as the eyes came up to meet his own.

"It—it's not Minelli, Mack," she told him haltingly, her soft voice coming to him through a fog of pain. "It's Marinello."

"What?"

He gripped her shoulders, released them when he realized he was causing her pain. The soldier's eyes were riveted with hers.

"He's Augie's son."

"Where *is* he, Sal?"

"I don't know." Sudden recognition, burning in the blue eyes like a cobalt flame. "Oh no, the *cars*."

Bolan didn't hear the rest. He was taking the stairs three at a time, sprinting through the hellgrounds toward a deadline he could not afford to miss.

A family reunion, right, with Grim Death serving as the host.

ERNESTO MARINELLO PUSHED ERITREA in front of him, his heavy Colt revolver prodding at the captive's back and urging him to greater speed. The smoky atmosphere of the narrow passageway was heavy with a smell of burning dreams.

It was only another fifty yards to the rear garage, where Marinello kept his backup wheels. The sleek Mercedes would be perfect, he decided. Power underneath the hood, and just enough room for himself, together with his ticket out.

Eritrea was coming with him, he decided; far enough to get him through the cordon that the police were throwing around the house. From the living room the sirens had been audible above the gunfire, and he had seen the flashing lights of cruisers circling the driveway, hemming in the tanks that had spearheaded the attack.

No point in wondering which family had betrayed him in his hour of triumph. There would be time enough for that when he was free and clear. To plot his comeback, right, and never mind the saying that you can't go home again.

He had achieved it once, or nearly so, and he would pull it off yet. His father's legacy was waiting for him, and he had already come too far, expended too much time and energy—too damn much money—to let it slip away without a fight.

Eritrea could help him there. The Feds and strike-force cops were jealous of their witnesses, and they would offer him safe conduct if he played it right. Then, once he cleared the cordon and was running safely...

Despite the smoke, Marinello smiled. He studied the back of Dave Eritrea's head, calculating where the bullet would go. He owed the bastard something, for the way he had moved in on Augie's territory when the old man bought it in New Jersey. Don Ernesto might have put it all together then, if only this one had not stepped in first and brought the whole damned Bolan mess right down around their ears. There had been chaos and disorder, territorial wars and prosecutions in Bolan's wake.

Marinello shrugged. His time was coming, and even the most bitter disappointment could not hold him off forever. It was coming, over Dave Eritrea's dead body.

Ahead of them, his pointman opened the person-sized door to the garage, giving them a breath of cleaner air as he stepped inside. He slapped the light switch with his palm, and brilliance filled the cavernous interior. Behind him, Marinello shoved Eritrea, propelling him inside.

"I'm taking the Mercedes," Marinello told his bodycock. "You get the door."

The gunner glanced inside the two-seater and frowned. There was a certain sluggishness as he did his *capo*'s bidding, reaching for the switch that would open the electric door and roll it back against the rafters.

"What about me, sir?" he finally asked.

"You won't be coming this time, Charley," Marinello answered. There was secret malice in his smile. "Somebody's got to keep an eye on things."

"You'll need a driver, Mr. Marinello."

"No, he won't."

The voice came to them from the darkness, just outside the open door, its tone invading Marinello's bones with ice. His bodycock was swiveling in the direction of the sound, and Marinello stepped across to stand behind Eritrea, one arm around the captive's throat, nestling the muzzle of his Colt against the pigeon's spine.

A black-clad figure stepped into the light, one arm outstretched, his fist wrapped tightly around the biggest goddamned silver hog leg Marinello ever saw. The muzzle, aimed directly at his face, looked big enough to fire a gold ball. A sheen of perspiration formed on the *capo*'s face and hands.

The guy was like no goddamned cop that he had ever seen before, and Marinello knew instinctively that he would have a tough time buying out of this one, with Eritrea or otherwise.

This guy was death, and he was there on business.

"Take him!" Marinello barked, and Charley made his move.

It wasn't even close.

The silver cannon swung across, the muzzle turning from Marinello to belch a tongue of fire directly in the hardman's face. Before the *capo*'s eyes, his head evaporated into crimson mist, the shards of bone and greasy droplets of his essence spraying over Marinello and Eritrea, small pieces of him clinging wetly to the mafioso's face, his suit. Then Bolan's weapon swung back to Marinello.

Held rigidly by Marinello, Eritrea eyed the man in black as if he was some kind of ghost. Marinello jammed his Colt against the pigeon's skull, forcing his head over sideways at an awkward angle, grinding steel against bone. He swallowed hard and tried to put steel in his voice.

"All right," he snarled, "so what's it gonna be?"

"YOUR HEAD," MACK BOLAN TOLD HIM SIMPLY.

"Yeah?"

There was a tremor in the mafioso's voice, but he stood firm, pressing his pistol tightly against Eritrea's skull.

"Suppose I give you this one and we call it even, eh?"

"No sale."

"Who's picking up the tab on this?"

"I've done a lot of business with your family," the soldier said. "Let's call it interest due."

The *capo* frowned, and he was looking for an answer in the middle of the maze when Dave Eritrea came out with it.

"Holy savior. Bolan."

Marinello shook his hostage violently.

"Cut out that shit," he growled. "You nuts, or what?"

But he turned to the warrior, and his cold eyes narrowed, searching Bolan's face. It was a face that neither he nor Dave Eritrea had ever seen before, and yet...

There might be something there, around the graveyard eyes...

The recognition hit him like a fist above the heart. Marinello lurched backward, dragging his human shield along for the ride.

"You're dead," he told the man in black.

"That's two of us, I guess."

The sweat on Marinello's brow glistened in the light.

"You took the old man out."

Bolan nodded. "Sorry you weren't there to see it."

"So am I. We could have saved some time."

"No time like the present, Ernie."

Marinello swallowed hard, searching for his voice and finally dredging it up from somewhere in his bowels.

"You want this piece of shit?" he asked, nodding toward Eritrea. "I'll give him to you for safe passage."

"I don't need safe passage," Bolan told him.

"Goddamn it, you know what I mean!"

"And I told you already, no sale."

Marinello's face was a study in stunned disbelief. "You'd kill him, just like that?"

The soldier shook his head. "You'll kill him. And then I'll kill you. Just like that."

Bolan ignored the whimpering sound coming from Dave Eritrea, concentrating on the Colt in Marinello's fist. He had the hammer down, but it was double action, and his mind was on the trigger pull, the time and energy that it would take to send a bullet burrowing into the captive's brain.

If he was swift and smooth enough...

The mafioso's face was going mottled, as if he was about to choke on something lodged in his throat.

"You don't leave me much choice," he whispered.

"None at all."

The move, when it came, had been sharpened to perfection in his mind before it was executed. A lifetime on the firing range and in the killgrounds was there behind it. The marksman was grimly determined as he crouched, extended the AutoMag in front of him and pointed at Marinello.

The first slug gored through his shoulder with all the impact of a rifle shot and would have come close to Dave Eritrea had he not collapsed to the floor. The would-be boss of bosses hurtled backward, glancing off the fender of a Mercedes and recoiling, falling to his knees, the six-inch Colt wobbling, spinning from his gun hand.

Bolan stood above the son of Augie Marinello, clearly panic-stricken, looking for some vestige of the father in his face—the old defiance, the bottled hatred, the desperation, the fiery vengefulness.

The old man wasn't there.

He never would be.

Bolan raised the AutoMag, sighted down the barrel and squeezed off three rounds in rapid fire. Marinello's face and eyes were vaporized on impact, and the headless straw man toppled slowly backward, folding in upon himself.

The Executioner stepped back, put the AutoMag down. Then he helped Dave Eritrea to his feet. At first the informer kept away from him, then saw the empty hand, accepted it, surprising Bolan with his strength, the firmness of his grasp.

"I never thought I'd see those eyes again," he said.

"You haven't," Bolan told him simply, making sure Eritrea understood.

"Right. Okay."

"Let's go," he said at last. "Your wife's waiting for you."

"Sure. And thanks."

Just that, no more. Nothing more was necessary, right.

Sarah Eritrea would be waiting for her husband, of course. Maybe there would be someone waiting for Mack Bolan, too.

The soldier thought of Sally Palmer. With any luck at all, they might now have time for that debriefing. God knows that it was overdue, for both of them.

And maybe this time they would get it right.

MORE ADVENTURE NEXT MONTH WITH

MACK BOLAN

#82 Hammerhead Reef

Fall of the drug lords

Mack Bolan answers a journalist's desperate cry
for help, but arrives in Florida to find the reporter
mysteriously murdered. And clues left by the man
lead to a billion-dollar drug empire.

Narcotics smugglers seem to be always one step
ahead of blockade attempts by U.S. agents. The
Executioner suspects someone in high circles is
leaking word to the drug runners. Bolan finally
corners the mastermind in a surprise showdown.

Enter the
'Gear Up For Adventure Sweepstakes'
You May Win a 1986 AMC Jeep® CJ
Off-road adventure — Only in a Jeep®

OFFICIAL RULES
No Purchase Necessary

1) To enter print your name, address and zip code on an Official Entry or on a 3″ x 5″ piece of paper. Enter as often as you choose but only one entry allowed to each envelope. Entries must be postmarked by January 17, 1986 and received by January 31, 1986. Mail entries first class. In Canada to Gold Eagle Gear Up For Adventure Sweepstakes, Suite 233, 238 Davenport Rd., Toronto, Ontario M5R 1J6. In the United States to Gold Eagle® Gear Up For Adventure Sweepstakes, P.O. Box 797, Cooper Station, New York, New York 10276. Sponsor is not responsible for lost, late, misdirected or illegibile entries or mail. Sweepstakes open to residents 18 years or older at entry of Canada (except Quebec) and the United States. Employees and their immediate families and household of Harlequin Enterprises Limited, their affiliated companies, retailers, distributors, printers, agencies, American Motors Corporation and RONALD SMILEY INC. are excluded. This offer appears in Gold Eagle publications during the sweepstakes program and at participating retailers. All Federal, Provincial, State and local laws apply. Void in Quebec and where prohibited or restricted by law.

2) First Prize awarded is a 1986 Jeep CJ with black soft top and standard equipment. Color and delivery date subject to availability. Vehicle license, driver license, insurance, title fees and taxes are the winner's responsibility. The approximate retail value is $8,500 U.S./$10,625 Canadian. 10 Second Prizes awarded of a Sports Binocular. The approximate retail value is $90 U.S./$112.50 Canadian. 100 Third Prizes awarded of Gold Eagle Sunglasses. The approximate retail value is $6.95 U.S./$8.65 Canadian. No substitution, duplication or cash redemption of prizes. First Prize distributed from U.S.A.

3) Winners will be selected in random drawings from all valid entries under the supervision of RONALD SMILEY INC. an independent judging organization whose decisions are final. Odds of winning depend on total number of entries received. First prize winner will be notified by certified mail and must return an Affidavit of Compliance within 10 days of notification. Winner residents of Canada must correctly answer a time-related arithmetical skill-testing question. Affidavits and prizes that are refused or undeliverable will result in alternate winners randomly drawn. The First Prize winner may be asked for the use of their name and photo without additional compensation. Income tax and other taxes are prize winners' responsibility.

4) For a major prize winner list, Canadian residents send a stamped, self addressed envelope to Gold Eagle Winner Headquarters, Suite 157, 238 Davenport Road, Toronto, Ontario M5R 1J6. United States residents send a stamped, self-addressed envelope to Gold Eagle Winner Headquarters, P.O. Box 182, Bowling Green Station, New York, NY 10274. Winner list requests may not include entries and must be received by January 31, 1986 for response.

A division of
WORLDWIDE LIBRARY®

DON PENDLETON'S EXECUTIONER

MACK BOLAN

Sergeant Mercy in Nam...The Executioner in the Mafia Wars...Colonel John Phoenix in the Terrorist Wars...Now Mack Bolan fights his loneliest war! You're never read writing like this before. By fire and maneuver, Bolan will rack up hell in a world shock-tilted by terror. He wages unsanctioned war—everywhere!

GOLD
EAGLE

Available wherever paperbacks are sold.

GET THE NEW WAR BOOK AND MACK BOLAN BUMPER STICKER FREE

Mail this coupon today!